OF PLAGUES AND BLASPHEMY

A MEDIEVAL HORROR ANTHOLOGY

GRAVE
BELLES

Of Plagues and Blasphemy: A Medieval Horror Anthology
Print edition ISBN: 979-8-9987736-2-4
E-book edition ISBN: 979-8-9987736-3-1

Published by Grave Belles Press of Grave Belles, LLC
www.gravebellespress.com

First edition: May 2026
10 9 8 7 6 5 4 3 2 1

CONTENTS

To all the voices that have been suppressed throughout history—then and now—we hear you.

Foreword

HISTORY HASN'T BEEN KIND to marginalized people. The medieval time period often conjures up castles, knights, and kings, but in truth, it was also a time when those in power restricted women and other individuals who didn't conform to rigid societal expectations. Many systems established then still influence modern struggles around gender, autonomy, and power.

When the stories in this anthology take place, women owning land was a rare occurrence. Significant pressure to conform to strict religious and social expectations around gender, reproduction, and marriage kept women and nonbinary persons trapped in a system where standing out resulted in violence and discrimination.

Their voices were silenced. History was distorted to forget their stories.

The injustice of this—important varied experiences being intentionally excluded from the historical record, filtered through religious doctrine or a pen held in the hand of a man—was the catalyst for this anthology, the first from Grave Belles Press.

This isn't just happening historically; it continues today. More than half the horror section of almost every bookstore is Stephen King or other male writers. It was discouraging to see so few female and non-binary voices take up space on those bookshelves. Art, whether written or visual, is meant to convey the complexity of our human experiences, and we see so many being left out of these spaces. How can one group of people tell the varied stories of others, especially when that group's privilege imparts a crucial bit of leverage to their very existence? The short answer is they can't.

So, we decided to do something about it.

We begin with this medieval anthology that you hold in your hands now. We were drawn to the potential horrors of the Dark Ages that could be told. There is so much that is horrific about those years, and all that people endured and perished from. That's where horror really writhes below your flesh–when you know it is an authentic experience of human history.

It's even more terrifying when those same horrors echo across centuries and you see it in the world around you today.

The pain of childbirth, the expectations of a woman, the chokehold of religion, the desperation for greatness, the suffocation of a loveless marriage, the lengths we are willing to go to survive or save the ones we love. These are all familiar to us now, and yet, these are the stories you will read through the pages of this book, set centuries before any of us drew breath.

Pull up a chair and grab a drink, or maybe a knife — whatever makes you feel safe. The female and non-binary authors found in these pages do more than just scare you with this collection...they take your heart and squeeze it tight, leaving you confronting dark truths within yourself and those around you.

Jess, Amanda, and Julia
March 2026

DEATH RITES OF AN ANCHORITE

SARATOGA SCHAEFER

T HERE IS A SPOT of mold on the bread. It creeps across the crust with lacy green fingers as if mimicking the lichen gripping the stone outside my window. I ponder scraping the mold off and eating the bread anyway. The accompanying stew is watery and swiftly growing chilled; Joan Giffard has interrupted my meal, as she often does this time of day, right before mass, but perhaps I should thank her. I might have missed the mold otherwise.

Eying the food on my tray, balanced on the small table pushed to the left side of the parlor window, I bite the inside of my cheek. My stomach clenches, remembering the rich, glistening meals I enjoyed at home, not even six months prior.

"Anchoress? Are you listening?" Joan's voice, pitched from nerves but just as treacly as ever, draws my attention back to her.

"I am here," I assure her, prodding the molded bread with a tentative finger. *Where else would I be?* There is nowhere for me to go. I am walled inside the church.

There's a soft sigh right outside my parlor window. I cannot see Joan. But her form, springy and thin like a sapling, is visible through the nearly translucent linen that hangs over the highest window in my anchorhold. The window is head height, and I'm not supposed to remove the curtain. I am dead to the world, after all. That does not stop the villagers from visiting, treating me like a confessional, sharing secrets and dreams, asking for advice. They think I am enlightened. They think I am wise and holy to forsake my life, and they talk to me in a way they cannot talk to Father Tilly. They do not know the truth.

I lean toward the window; there's an odd smell lingering on the breeze, like pig skin crisping over a fire. If Joan left, I could move the curtain, look for the source of the scent. When no one else is around, I twitch the linen to the side and peer out, studying the church's graveyard, the copse of trees directly in front of my anchorhold, the slithering dirt path that leads into the village. I yearn to feel the sun on my cheeks before it slips over the top of the building, unreachable until tomorrow. The anchorhold is on the north side of the church; I will get little sunlight once winter arrives in a month. Soon I will add thicker, oiled cloth to the exterior-facing windows to block the chill.

My first winter sealed up. My first winter free.

"Richard is behaving strangely," Joan continues, unaware of my wavering attention. "I would be a good wife to him. But how can I when he avoids me? When he chews the side of his fingers until they bleed? He has been silent. Has closed the smithy with no reason, and we need the coin. He does not sleep. He stares at the ceiling and smiles, eyes empty. He did not do that before, but I cannot understand what has changed."

I suppress a sigh. Richard may be ill, and Joan expects assistance. I have not yet adjusted to this role; I thought it would be far more solitary. I did not realize anchorites were the keepers of wagging tongues, the repository for the village's secrets and gossip.

"Our Lord has showed me Lady Saint Mary," I offer, trying to keep my voice calm and reverent. "Three times: with Child, in sorrow under the cross, and as she is now, filled with joy. Perhaps you and Richard are under the cross. You must take Lady Saint Mary into your heart. Let her guide you."

There is silence on the other side of the curtain. I worry my lip between my teeth, twisting my fingers together, glancing again at the table, at my moldy bread and lukewarm stew.

"You are truly blessed," Joan says eventually. "As am I to receive such advice."

"I will pray for you both," I reply, knowing it's what Joan wants to hear. She is one of my more frequent visitors, usually fretting over how her womb has not yet quickened despite being married to Richard Giffard for a year now.

Joan lets out a choked sob. "Dear Anchoress, thank you."

I flinch at the title. My clothing is simple and plain, fashioned for warmth and utility instead of status or aesthetic, but it tethers me to the life I tried to leave behind. A coal-colored kirtle and a white wimple; in winter I will add a pilch to keep me warm. The kirtle is shapeless and loose, a welcome relief from the tighter gowns I wore in my father's house. But still the clothes of a woman.

Joan cannot know how I wish they would all call me anchorite instead. The village has seen my body and presume I belong within it, bestowing on me the title of anchoress—a good woman who has withdrawn from the world, embracing Our Lord through a life of solitary prayer and contemplation.

I do not belong here. But I do not belong out there even more, so I will accept the name, the misunderstanding. Because at least I have avoided a life of marriage, of being a bride, of motherhood. Of being forced to reside in this role that does not fit, that never fit. In here, I am safe.

I do not understand what I am, neither man nor woman, a soul trapped in a body much more confining than an anchorhold. Our Lord has not always been kind to me, but perhaps under His roof, I will learn myself.

At the very least, here, I know I am free.

Just shy of my eighteenth year, my parents were getting impatient. I was behind. My younger brother William was already betrothed to a lass up north, though he was six years my junior. When I told my parents I wanted to commit myself to the church instead, become an anchorite, my father was pleased enough. It got me out of the house, out of his way, and in good standing with the church—he would be my patron, paying for my keep.

My mother, on the other hand, was reluctant.

"Are you certain?" she asked, calling me by the name she bestowed upon me at birth, the one I cast aside when I entered the anchorhold. I refer to myself as the anchorite now, a safe designation. "They will seal you inside the anchorhold. You cannot leave save by special permission. You will never have a husband. Or children. Do not be hasty with this decision."

It was a conversation I would have again, several weeks later, with Bishop Becker, since those intent on becoming anchorites were interviewed to make sure they were of sound mind.

Bishop Becker was a stout man with close-set eyes and a moustache like a fox tail. He shifted at our dining table, gratefully sipping the wine a servant procured for him, watching me with beady fascination.

"You understand you will be dead?" he asked. I could not draw my eyes from his moustache, the wiry rust-colored hairs that drooped toward his lips, as if they were trying to crawl inside the wet, dark warmth of his mouth. "I will read your Rites. You will be sealed in the anchorhold. You will die there. Your life will be dedicated to mental silence, prayer, and mortification."

I told him I understood. I told him I was eager to subdue my body's earthly desires and pledge myself to Our Lord.

"You must work to be as little fond of your windows as possible," Bishop Becker continued. "The parlor window especially. That is where people will come to seek counsel. Though you will be deceased, your duty is to act as an intermediary for the congregation. You cannot betray the confidences of anyone who comes to you."

"Yes, I understand."

It was not hard to convince him. I grew up going to daily mass, listening to Father Tilly's homilies. The private tutor afforded to me by my father was fluent in religious instruction. I learned to read the Bible, copy out passages, embroider linens and cloths, sew, and complete simple mathematics. I was not a peasant looking to escape a life of backbreaking labor and callused palms.

I am the eldest child of William M. Ludlow, a perfect fit for the anchorhold.

The day Bishop Becker performed my death rites, the day I was sealed in the anchorhold, I cried. Not from fear, hearing the scraping of the mortar as they bricked up the entrance. Not from regret, casting my gaze around the tiny room, only big enough to hold a small table, chair, lumpy mattress, and chamber pot. No, I cried from relief. The hot tears rolled silently down my raised cheeks, and I smiled at the darkness.

When Joan leaves, silence descends again, blissful and thick. I pick at the bread, avoiding the molded bits, and slurp the cold stew. I say a few quick prayers for Joan Giffard and her husband, then place the tray near the low window, within easy reach. Cicily, the servant my father's patronage pays for, will take it away later.

The anchorhold has four limestone walls—one of those walls shared with the church—and three windows. The parlor window faces the churchyard. A second window, more of an opening, really, is lower to the ground on the east wall. The third is the squint, a small window that connects my anchorhold to the church.

I glance around at my straw-stuffed mattress, which took some getting used to after the downy bed in my father's house, the chamber pot, which Cicily emptied early today, and the scuffed table. It is not a bad life. Not when you compare it with what I left behind.

Shuffling over to the western corner, I lift the skirts of my kirtle and kneel before the grave, nestled only a meter from my mattress. I should be praying, but I prefer digging. As a result, the grave is already quite deep, several feet of earth missing. My hands sink into the soil, cold and dry.

There is a scraping at the low window, and I turn in time to see Eadmund enter, his ropey black tail brushing against the stone. He sniffs at the tray, rearing back, offended by the lack of meat, and stalks deeper into the anchorhold, meowing plaintively, as if I am secretly hoarding food.

"I am sorry, I have nothing," I explain to him, holding up my dirty hands. Sprinkles of soil rain down my sleeves, collecting at the elbows of my kirtle. "I am rarely given meat, my friend."

Eadmund does not need me to feed him. He comes and goes as he pleases, easily accessing the lower window, pouncing on fieldmice in the graveyard and stalking birds in the trees.

"You cannot have jewelry or sumptuous foods. No one else is allowed in the anchorhold," Bishop Becker explained during our interview. "You may, however, have a cat for company."

Eadmund was already a tenant of the graveyard, one of several strays that lurked outside the church. When I was sealed inside, the cat began to visit; slipping into the low window, getting comfortable on my bed, licking the hard cheese Cicily served.

Eadmund mews again, dragging his cheek against my skirts, then leaps away to the bed, kneading the wool blanket, yawning, curling his body into a knot of black.

Mass is starting soon, so I shift the handfuls of dirt I cleaved from the bottom of the grave to the side, stamp them down against the packed floor. I am supposed to consider the grave, pray over it. Remove a few fistfuls of dirt a day and pass them to Cicily through the servant window. I am not supposed to fixate, obsess. But when my fingers grow tired from embroidering altar cloths, I sink my hands into the earth. It is better than praying for hours. Even if I am digging my own grave.

I always wonder if there is another anchorite in this room. Under my feet. Their body decayed and wispy with death. No one told me. I do not know the last time an anchorite lived here.

From the church comes a clear, high voice. A second weaves around the first, adding texture. A third, baritone, joins, giving the hymn a belly.

I brush my hands off and navigate around the mattress, kneeling on the hard ground before the squint. A thin, vertical window, barely large enough to fit my fist through, slits from the anchorhold, offering a view into the church. Father Tilly is flitting around the altar, cloaked in white and gold. The church smells of incense and wax and the ripeness of the bodies in the pews.

I must be physically present for this. Watch the service. Take communion. Appear every inch the holy woman they think I am. But as my knees grow numb and Father Tilly begins to speak, my mind wanders.

Through the squint, I scan the familiar faces. Sometimes I see Mother, Father, and William, though they have taken to sitting in the far back, away from my squint. I crane my neck, pressing a check against the cool stone, but I cannot spot them today.

They do not visit me. Perhaps it is too difficult. I miss William, and sometimes Mother. I cannot fault them for being uneasy coming to me for spiritual advice. Perhaps that will change in a few years when I am less a person and more a part of the church, like a piece of stained glass. When I am further away from the expectations placed on the form I found myself in at birth.

When I turned twelve, my body started to change, rebelling in ways I did not consent to. It wasn't just the buds on my chest or the fine hair between my legs. It was the concept behind it. I felt not like a lady at all. Nor a man. Anything I did was a farce. A performance. It was not *real*. I could not imagine lying with a man or giving birth. It felt almost perverse, bone-chilling. I wondered if there was some third role I could discover, a place that let me stretch outside the boundaries of these two spaces, but though I looked, it did not seem to exist. I chose the anchorhold instead.

My mind slows, sputters to a stop, as my eyes land on a pair of children in the front pew. They sit, intertwined, ankles hooked around each other, staring rapturously at Father Tilly. The Dodd twins. John Dodd and Mary Dodd frame their children, ramrod straight, taking pride in their spot at the front. They are not watching their sons. They do not see Ralph with his index finger between his front teeth or Hugh cramming his hand into the small cavern of his mouth. No one but me notices as both twins bite down at the same time, slips of blood dribbling from their lips. The boys withdraw their hands, gouges in their skin. Crimson sluggishly pools from tiny tears made by their baby teeth.

I nearly scream as something heavy lands on my shoulder. But it's only Eadmund, balancing like a bird on a branch. He purrs in my ear, leaning forward to peer out the squint.

His weight pulls me to the side—has he always been this heavy?—but I return my attention to the Dodd boys in time to see them wordlessly reach for each other. Ralph sticks his bloody finger between Hugh's lips; Hugh allows Ralph to suckle from his gnawed knuckles. The twins do not look at each other. They are fixed upon Father Tilly, bloody hands in each other's mouths, sucking mindlessly.

My stomach lurches, soggy stewed vegetables threatening to reappear.

Eadmund purrs louder, rubs his face against my cheek, and leaps to the ground, trotting out the lower window. I lean closer to the squint, hands clammy against the frame. A bead of blood, glistening in the candlelight, rolls from the corner of Ralph's mouth and drops in his lap, silent and unnoticed to all but me.

Something wakes me.

The night smells of ice and fresh soil, the moon nearly full, casting pearly light upon the churchyard.

I retired early, resolving to mention the twins to Father Tilly if I observed anything like that again. Perhaps it was an odd quirk; or perhaps the isolation is affecting me already. I have only been in the anchorhold since May, but Bishop Becker warned me that if I did not keep to my prayers and religious study, my mind might play tricks on me, being confined to such a small space.

Did I dream of the twins? Of their bloody mouths? Is that what woke me?

"Hail!"

I jump, the wool blanket slipping off my shoulders, exposing my skin to the crisp night air leaking in through the windows.

"W-who approaches?" The words fight me on their way out, dry and sticking to the roof of my mouth.

"Anchorite? Are you in there?"

I sit up, the blanket falling away. I am unsure of the time, but it is quiet, late. The voice comes from the curtained window. The moon is bright enough to silhouette a visitor's form, but there is nothing there. I could light a candle, but the thought of striking a flint, the harshness of the sound, makes me hesitant.

There is a peculiar smell, like animal pelts over a fire or skin crisping after an unpleasant burn. Did I not smell that earlier today too?

"Hail," the visitor says again, and this is what woke me. The voice is thinly pitched, but layered, as if there are multiple voices woven into one.

I wrap the blanket tightly around my shoulders. The visitor can't see me, but it is improper, me without my kirtle, feet bare, hair loose. I remember Bishop Becker's warning.

"You will be speaking mostly with women," he said. "If any man requests to see you, ask him what good might come of it. There are...temptations. Evils. You must be ready and willing to shut the window quickly on any man who is immoderate."

"It would be my pleasure," I replied before I could think better of it.

Someone coming to my window in the dead of night is exactly what Bishop Becker was afraid of. The evils. The temptations.

"Who is out there?" I say, fingers digging into the wool fabric.

"Do not be startled!" the voice reassures. "I have only come to ask a question." The voice lilts and twists, as if coming from first the left side of the parlor window, then the right.

I inch forward, drawn to the curtain, but stop when a draft from behind breathes against my neck. I glance over my shoulder at the squint. It's like peering into the slitted mouth of a beast. The altar is not visible from here; I could get closer, find the shadowy ridges of the pews, but I balk. The squint's opening is small, yet I have the sudden sense that if I go over there, something will appear underneath it, pulling me through into the church.

I blink, staggering backward to the parlor window.

"Why do you come to my window so late?" I ask, reluctantly turning from the squint and sidling next to the parlor window. There is no sign of the speaker, though the moon lights up the anchorhold, illuminating the half-dug grave in the corner.

"I did not wish for us to be interrupted," the voice says, a sharp, satisfied snap to the tone, like icicles breaking. "My friend told me I could find you here. Do you enjoy it?"

I hug the blanket tighter to my chest. "Pardon?"

The voice sighs. "This. Do you enjoy this? Being an anchorite?"

Distantly, I note the voice has called me an anchorite twice now instead of anchoress. "I am honored and blessed to serve Our Lord in such a way."

"You did not answer the question," the voice says, slightly amused. Then, suddenly, as if the speaker is much closer, pressing a mouth against the bars of the window, "Do you enjoy it?"

I want to twitch the curtain to the side, reveal the speaker. For this voice does not belong to a villager. I grew up here; I know the voices, can recognize bodies and faces through the thin curtain. This speaker is not anyone I am familiar with. And I cannot find their shadow, cannot pinpoint their form behind the fabric.

"I do," I finally say, hoping this will be enough, hoping the speaker will go.

"Would you ever leave?" Now the voice sounds like it's coming from the wall I am pressed against, slithering in through the cracks in the stones.

"I would need permission to leave," I reply, twisting my fingers against the rough wool, rubbing until the fabric hurts.

"But would you?"

"No," I say honestly. "You may see a cell, but I am free here. And I have dedicated myself to Our Lord, who I am honored to serve," I add quickly.

"Very interesting," the voice says. "Thank you, anchorite. Have a pleasant evening."

There's a soft scuffling outside the parlor window, and I lurch forward, releasing the blanket with one hand and pressing my palm against the cold stone. "Wait! Who are you? Who told you to come to me?"

But this time, there is no answer.

"He is getting worse, Anchoress," Joan says, wavering in front of the curtain. "Please, help us."

She arrived at daybreak, interrupting what was supposed to be my morning prayers, which I had no energy for after being up half the night. After the speaker left, I tossed and turned, skin chilled, fingers frozen, even as I hunkered under the blanket. After some time, Eadmund appeared at my side, curling against my hip. His steady purrs and warm weight finally allowed me to drift off.

A traveler. Someone passing through who was curious about the anchorhold. Nothing more. I cannot dwell on last night's visitor, not now that Joan is back, nearly frantic. Richard has begun to speak in "strange tongues," his eyes nearly lifeless, his hands bloody. Joan's words make me think of the Dodd twins, of their own bloody hands, and I shiver. I hope there is not a sickness spreading. A pox would burn through this village.

"Perhaps you should speak with Father Tilly," I suggest, fighting back a yawn that creaks against my jaw. "In the meantime, I will pray for Richard." I bite back guilt. I did not do much praying yesterday.

When Joan leaves, sniffing back tears, Cicily knocks on the stone above the low window. "Hail, Anchoress." She slides a tray into the anchorhold—more flavorless vegetable stew, a hunk of cheese, and a heel of bread.

"Cicily," I call out before she can move away, ignoring the tray. "Are there any travelers about? Passing merchants or traders? Anything of the sort?"

Cicily is silent for a moment. I cannot see her, but I imagine her weathered, lined face, crinkled blue eyes, the way she chews on a fingertip when thinking. "No, Anchoress. None that are known to me."

Eadmund, woken by the clatter of the tray, marches over to the servant window and swipes at the cheese, needling his claws into the rind and gnawing the nutty tip, splashing saliva across the surface.

Cicily empties my chamber pot and returns it, then leaves as I nibble the bread and sip the lukewarm stew. Eadmund leaves, off to hunt for a second breakfast, no doubt. I will work on my embroidery today—an altar cloth with shining gold thread depicting angels and trumpets. I will pray. I will be a good anchorite.

But when whispers echo from the squint, I cannot help myself. I glance inside the church—Joan Giffard listened to my suggestion. She stands near the pulpit with Father Tilly, both their voices hushed and made mellifluous by the arched ceiling and wooden beams. Joan's shoulders are tight, hunched around her ears, her gaze caught on the hem of Father Tilly's robe. Hands clasped, she presses her fists against her chest as if she could drive them into her heart.

Father Tilly looms over Joan. He is a sallow-faced man with white spider fingers and long arms, as if stretched from his shoulders like hot tallow. His jaw is nearly concave, eyes hidden in the shadows from the pulpit. He reaches for Joan, long fingers draping against her shoulder.

I am unseen. Anchorites do not eavesdrop. Neither of them thinks to glance at the squint, and the early morning is cloudy, obscuring the anchorhold in a swirl of gloom.

Father Tilly's voice lifts, rumbles, then lowers. Joan carefully looks up, catching his eye, then swiftly glances away again. Father Tilly's hand creeps from her shoulder to her neck, where he briefly strokes her jawline, the bob of her throat, before heaving his fingers away.

Joan appears to be crumpling, a used handkerchief scrunched in a fist, but Father Tilly's expression is almost hungry. He claps his other hand against Joan's back, nods, and strides away, swallowed up by the church. Joan is frozen for a moment, then shudders back to life, scurrying out through the front doors.

I swallow hard. I expected Father Tilly to be comforting, but the way he touched Joan was...unnerving. My palms are slick against the squint, throat dry. I suppress a shudder.

From behind me, comes the voice: "Hail, anchorite."

I rear from the church window, spinning to face the parlor, pushing all thoughts of Father Tilly and Joan aside. "Is it you? Are you back?"

"I had another question," the voice says cheerfully. Twined with high and low tones, it is difficult to say if I am speaking with a man or a woman.

I am not usually allowed to draw back the curtain. It is there to remind people that I am capable of counsel and religious instruction but not one of them. Not of this world. Dead and given to the church. But there are exceptions.

I step to the very edge of the parlor window, but still cannot see the speaker.

"You may ask your question," I say, and I twitch aside the curtain, giving myself a gap to peer out of.

For a moment, I am overwhelmed by the murky sunlight, the dappled trees, the corner of the graveyard. I occasionally look out the window, but every time I do, I am struck, frozen, as if I have forgotten there's more than these four walls and the grave at my feet.

"If you wanted to see me, you only had to ask," the voice remarks, pulling me back to my task.

I tear my eyes from the iron sky and falling leaves, the scent of wheat and hay on the breeze. But I cannot find the speaker. The window's views are uninterrupted.

"Down here."

I press closer to the window, shifting the curtain to the side, gazing down.

A child. But a disquieting one, for the child's body faces the anchorhold while his head faces the copse of trees. The child is far shorter than the parlor window. No wonder I could not see him last night.

"What is your name?" I whisper, mouth dry and scratchy.

"That is not of much importance," the child says, voice lilting.

The child wears a long tunic, dark breeches, no shoes. His hair is a soft brown, like rabbit's fur, tumbling down in buoyant curls. His dress is familiar, and he shares the same accent as the rest of the village.

Except this child is wrong.

His head is perched on his body backwards, face turned to the woods, impossible to see his expression or features. The child does not appear to be in pain or discomfort despite the unnatural twist in his neck; he stands easily underneath the window, hands gently folded in front of the shabby tunic, toes stained with dirt. A smell rises, like that of burning meat.

This child belongs to no one, the thought comes, rising like a fog, chilling my bones. I have the urge to flee, to put as much distance between me and this…creature as possible, but there is nowhere to go.

"The people here," the child says, tipping his head up, brown curls bouncing. "What are they like?"

My face feels feverish and hot. I swallow a froth of sputum that has grown in the back of my throat. "They are good people," I cough. "Good and holy."

I cannot see the smile, for the child's face is turned backward, neck twisted like thread around a finger, but I hear the curve of lips in his response. "Excellent."

The child walks backward without any effort, never turning his head around, striding with much longer steps than should be possible for his short stature. Before vanishing into the trees, he lifts an arm and waves.

Panting against the window, I glance at the graveyard, catching sight of Eadmund perched on a headstone, washing a paw.

I wrench the curtain closed, fingers tingling, and drop to my knees in the dirt, dragging myself to the grave, thrusting my hands into the earth. Prayers fall from my lips, rubied, frantic, but I can barely hear them over the scrape of dirt. The burning flesh smell remains, sticking to the inside of my nose. The anchorhold tightens around me, a womb of stone.

The child stays away for two days, but so does Joan. I became accustomed to her visits, and when I ask Cicily if Joan is well, my servant has no response. She passes me food and empties my chamber pot, but she does not speak, and finally I stretch out on the floor so I can look up at Cicily from the low window. Her blue eyes are glassy, lined face slack. She does not notice me reaching for her, calling her name.

Yesterday Father Tilly tried to give communion to Margery Crump and she bit him. He yelped, anger flashing across his face, but collected himself, praying over her, and then forcing the bread down her throat. The congregation did not react, though I expected titters or soft gasps. The church was silent and observant, something that continues today.

I open my mouth to receive communion through the squint. Father Tilly usually comes to me first before the rest of the congregation. He smells of hay and myrrh, his fingers damp as he places the Body of Christ upon my waiting tongue. He looks at me, eyes trailing to my neck, and I wish I could disappear into the wimple, puddle down inside my kirtle.

Father Tilly has never looked at me like this before. Most of the time he barely notices me, shoving communion into the squint's opening and then turning back to his flock. But now he lingers near the opening, long fingers trailing on the stone before heading back to the altar.

"My children," he declares, "The eternal punishment of hell might yet be escaped with commitment to the Lord, union with Christ."

The congregation is slumped, some people hunched over, as if they are going to be sick. Margery Crump is in the second pew, next to her husband, drooling into her lap. The Dodd twins are visible in the first row, but the whole family—mother, father, boys—are slack-jawed, eyes empty and wide. Their knuckles are crusted over with dried blood.

I lean forward as far as I can and spot Joan and Richard Giffard a few pews behind the Dodds. They are both perfectly still but drooping forward, faint smiles on their faces. I try to catch Joan's eye, beckon her over, but she is limp and unseeing.

Father Tilly gestures for the congregation to line up for communion, but no one moves. He looks confused, fingers flexing against the ciborium. Tries again. Then Margery Crump rises unsteadily, a weed in the wind, and walks down the aisle, the front doors slamming behind her.

One by one, the congregation stands and trickles out of the church. Father Tilly stares, mouth ajar, as if he has forgotten himself completely.

"He goes to the next town over, you know."

I pull away from the squint, rushing over to the parlor window, yanking the curtain to the side. I am too vicious with it; the curtain tears clean off, fluttering to the ground. The child chuckles, very close to the anchorhold's exterior wall, the top of his head visible. The child is tilting his chin to the ground so that the back of his head is turned up, hiding his face. The child's hands are pressing against the stone. His fingers are too clean. Too white. Like the belly of a fish.

"Please leave us alone," I beg.

"He goes to the next town over," the child repeats. "He visits places where he can find women. He leaves them leaning against buildings or splayed out in fields. He mashes their throats with his lovely strong fingers."

My stomach twists, and I fight back a gag.

"Then he comes back here and puts his hands in your mouth. In all of their mouths." The child giggles, a cracking, frostbitten sound. A slip of darkness flits from the graveyard to the anchorhold, winding through the child's legs. The child dips, stroking a hand along Eadmund's spine. "Hello, friend."

The cat purrs, then slinks around the anchorhold, entering through the serving window. Sniffing at me once, Eadmund comes to sit near my open grave, watching me with bulbous yellow eyes.

"Our Lord in Heaven…" I whisper, the prayer trailing off weakly.

"I am afraid not," the child laughs, pulling his hands away from the anchorhold.

The child scampers off backward, racing toward the treeline, the stench of sizzling skin wafting after him.

I shove Eadmund to the side; the cat spits and hisses, but I cannot soothe him. The hole beckons me. My hands sink deep in the earth, digging.

I wait by the window, hoping for a villager to pass. Hoping to see Cicily with my evening meal. But no one comes, and the evening cold drives me to bed, to the wool blanket and Eadmund's warmth.

The sounds of sawing, clattering, snapping wake me the next morning. I lurch from bed, nearly tripping into my grave, hurriedly pulling on my kirtle and slamming against the parlor window, now bared to the world. I catch sight of Cicily wandering past the anchorhold, arms full of logs.

"Cicily!" I cry, stretching my arm out from the barred window. "Cicily, please! Something is terribly wrong. We need to warn people."

The servant glances my way, eyes blank and hooded. A slow, luxurious smile unfurls across her face. "There is no need for that, anchorite."

I freeze. The voice is familiar, but not in the way I expect. "There is a great evil here."

Cicily nods. "Indeed. It is time to cast it out."

"No," I whisper, arm wilting against the stone window. "No, I speak of the thing that comes from the woods—"

"It is nearly over, anchorite," Cicily says, amicably. "Be still now." She hurries across the churchyard, carrying her logs toward the front of the building.

I spin, running to the squint, gasping to see the church already full of people. There is tinder everywhere. Logs, branches, snapped sticks, broken chairs. The villagers, dead-eyed and slouching, toss more kindling around the church, surrounding the pews, anointing the altar. The church is made of limestone, but there is wood everywhere— beams, arches, roof, scaffolding. The villagers are only helping along what will come naturally, given the right nudge.

"No!" I scream through the squint. "You must not do this!"

No one hears me, or no one cares. Familiar faces stand out in the crowd: my family.

"Mother, Father, William!" I call. "Will you not hear my voice? Please break yourself from this!"

But my family's features are blank and smooth, like pebbles from the river. Bloody marks stain their fingers. They drop armfuls of tinder in the aisle, then take their seats near the front of the church. Slowly, the other villagers follow, arranging their kindling and sinking into the pews.

Commotion from the back of the church rings through the space, but I cannot get a good look from here. I plaster my hands against the squint, wondering if I can fold myself up like a strip of paper and slide through the opening. But no. None of the windows in the anchorhold are large enough for a body to get through.

"Help!" I cry, but my voice is drowned out by Father Tilly, coming into view, being dragged up the aisle by five strong men.

Father Tilly thrashes, a keening coming from his throat, but the men who grip him are wooden, minds faraway, hands locked around the priest's limbs and hair. They force him up to the altar, the rest of the congregation patiently waiting in their pews.

A hum begins, first from the floor, then from the throats of the villagers. My mother opens her mouth and sings the words of a song I do not recognize. My father joins, then William. Then the Dodds, in their usual spot. Margery Crump carries the tune higher, and soon the whole church is singing, but it is not a language I have ever heard before. The melody is discordant, the words are nonsense. As if someone was speaking backward.

As the song spirals louder, four of the men pin Father Tilly to the altar's table, tearing at his robes, exposing his pale body. The fifth man reaches for the chrismaria, the silver-gilt container holding consecrated oil, and cracks the lid open on the altar. He pours the oil on Father Tilly, soaking his face, chest, genitals, and the remnants of his robes, fat globules flying through the air.

I cannot scream; my voice is gone, my breath tucked in my chest. I cannot do anything but watch, be the witness the church expected when I was sealed away.

Soft footsteps echo down the aisle—Joan Giffard comes into view, carrying a torch, stepping lightly around piles of tinder. The song lifts around her, swaddling her, reaching the very corners of the church.

There's a resounding crash as the doors slam shut.

Joan reaches the altar, looks down at Father Tilly, writhing against the men holding him on the table. Her smile is bland, calm. The fire bathes her features in pulsing orange light.

The song crests, peaks, and stops suddenly, crashing, leaving nothing in its wake.

Joan touches the torch to Father Tilly's neck. The flame jumps eagerly, tongue licking across his throat and up to his hair before racing down his chest to consume his entire body. His scream is unearthly, all-consuming, but chokes out quickly as the fire wraps burning hands around his neck.

The men step back from the table, releasing Father Tilly, chivalrously escorting Joan to an open spot at a pew in the front. As they take their seats, the church silent save for the crackling fire on Father Tilly's body, the priest thrashes, rolling from the table to the floor. He scrambles upright, his body a bright, blistering flame, and tries to stagger down the aisle, perhaps hoping to get outside. He does not make it, the fire already consuming his body, his head a white-hot beacon. Father Tilly jerks to the floor, hidden by the pews, smoke spiraling up from his body.

As soon as the priest is down, Joan lets her torch drop to the floor, where the fire meets straw and sticks and chews them hungrily. Flames lick up the wooden pew, spreading quickly, angrily.

"Run!" I yell to the congregation. "Get out now!"

But they do not listen. They stare ahead, at the altar, as if listening to a homily, hands in their laps, expressions vacant. They do not move, do not speak, as their clothing catches fire, their hair going up in flame. Skin bubbles and eyes fry in their sockets.

Joan burns. Cicily burns. The Dodd twins burn. My family burns. The villagers—everyone who lives here, people I have known my entire life—burn.

The fire is spreading, blasting a sheet of heat at me, smoke coiling through the squint. Stones crack, the church's roof catches on fire. Everything is quiet except for the beams groaning and wood sizzling. The smell of burning flesh floods the anchorhold. Familiar. Searing.

I wheel away from the squint as something large falls from the church's ceiling. The whole building is going to collapse. Smoke pours into the anchorhold, seizing my lungs, and I look around wildly as if hoping the bricked-up door will suddenly open.

"Hail, my friend," says a familiar voice, high over the sounds of the church burning.

I plant myself against the parlor window. The child is standing a few feet away, head resolutely turned toward the woods. Eadmund the cat is perched on the child's shoulder, tail waving lazily, his eyes bright, reflecting the burning building.

"Why did everyone have to die if the only sinner was Father Tilly?" I yell through the window, tears mixing with phlegm as I cough, the smoke stinging my eyes.

"Do you truly believe no one else knew what he was doing?" the child asks, cocking his head to one side. "Do you believe those who did not know would do anything if they did?"

"I did not know," I hack out. "And I would have done something."

The child laughs. "Here? In your cell?" The child's head tilts back to center, and he takes a step forward. "It is no matter. I believe you. And I have a deal for you, dear anchorite. You can stay here, be crushed under the church or choked by the smoke. Or you can come with me. You can be mine."

I am not the most devout Christian. I am not the perfect anchorite, joining for holy reasons and dedicating my life to the Lord's work. I am in this room for selfish reasons, but those reasons came about because I have been forced into a ruthless world, one that does not allow room for people like me. But it was my choice. My burden. And I would rather die in this body than be tricked into a worse state by this creature.

"No," I say, and my voice is steady and clear, even as smoke furls inside my chest.

"No?" the child mocks. "Foolish."

"You killed my family," I hiss.

The child's shoulders lift up toward his ears. "Had to be done. Well then, I shall say my goodbyes." The child's head starts to turn.

Eadmund gives a disgruntled mew at the movement and jumps down, pattering away to the graveyard.

I do not know much, but I do know that I cannot see this creature's face. I catch a glimpse of a ridged cheek, a slick of forehead, and then I fling myself away from the window. The anchorhold is thick with smoke and the church is grinding, crackling, the smell of charred skin a heavy fug in the air.

There is only one place to go. Down.

I throw myself into the grave, burrowing, and the child's laughter peals in through the open window. I scoop the fresh dirt Cicily never collected over my body. It is easier to breathe down here, four feet beneath the thick smoke, and I hurriedly shovel soil on my lower half and chest, knocking down the tops of the earthy walls so they cover me.

I do not know what is next. Perhaps the fire will peter out and I will survive, and a passing traveler will hear my cries and release me.

Or perhaps the anchorhold will collapse, flattening me. Or I will starve to death, trapped under the rubble. Or I will bury myself too well, suffocating. Either way, I will make it easy for anyone who finds me. This is my grave. I was always going to end up here.

I disappear into the earth, into my home, and a rush fills my body—a release, a becoming. Darkness descends as the ringing laughter of the child fades away. The smell of loam blots out the acerbic burning flesh. Soil gets in my mouth, becomes mud on my tongue, and I swallow, hungry for holy dirt.

THE HEART, THE HUNT

M. STEVENSON

MY HUSBAND AND THE first snow arrive together; both are early.

The sound of hooves on the road is muffled by the falling flakes, and I barely pull myself together in time to greet him: hair bound and concealed under my wimple, dress straight and clean, face blank as if it has never been marked by emotions he would find unbecoming. My heart speeds as I hasten down the stairs from the keep, emerging just in time to see him riding through the gates flanked by a dozen cloaked men. The shine of his armor strikes my eyes like a blow, but I cannot—dare not—look away.

Isabeau stands behind me, close enough that I can feel her warmth against my back. If only we could go back to this morning—to when I woke at dawn to her nose pressed to my nape, our fingers tangled together, blissfully ignorant of the storm that was already coming. I wrap my rosary around my fingers to stop myself from reaching for her hand, because while to anyone else it would look meaningless—the lady of the castle leaning on her loyal handmaiden, overcome by the sight of her lord returning at last from the holy war—part of me is afraid that *he* will know.

Maybe, I dare to think as he dismounts, swinging a leg over the back of his destrier. Maybe it will not be so bad. It has been seven years, after all, since he rode off at the king's side; people can change in seven years.

He looks across the courtyard and his eyes find mine, dark and cold as old iron.

A shiver runs through me that I cannot blame on winter's arrival.

He has not changed. Of course he has not changed.

Robert, lord of the Château du Bois—the man everyone save Isabeau and I know as my husband—strides across the castle yard. He comes close to me, closer, closer still, and I resist the urge to step back as he occupies my vision until his face is all I can see.

"Agnès," he says. His voice is low, horribly intimate.

My fist clenches on my rosary. No one but Isabeau has said my Christian name in so long that it feels like a profanity. An invasion of a place I had thought private.

Robert's gaze flicks down to my balled-up hand. The corners of his mouth deepen as he reaches for it. His hand is gloved, and that is the only thing that prevents me from flinching as he takes my fist and pries my bloodless fingers open.

The rosary drops to the ground before I think to catch it.

Robert raises my hand to his mouth. He brushes his lips across my knuckles. Chaste. Pure. Chivalrous. Of course he is all those things when everyone is watching. His mouth is deceptively soft, his breath animal-hot on my fingers.

"Milady," he says louder, for those assembled to hear.

Wind shrieks around the ramparts, or perhaps it is the cry of the beast at hunt, seeking another victim. Robert's gaze flicks up, and he releases my hand. It falls limp back to my side, as if I've lost control of my own limbs.

The rosary's carmine beads gleam up at me, drops of blood against the bone-white snow.

Of course I knew it was possible that he would return. I can even lie to myself and say I hoped he would, that I prayed for his safety when I learned the French army had been captured in the Holy Lands along with the king.

But I would have made the perfect widow: too grief-stricken, everyone would say, to consider marrying again.

As the sun bites the horizon, I prepare to go down to supper. Clean overdress. Rosary on my wrist, silver cross around my neck, girdle around my waist. I cannot seem to fasten the girdle: my fingers are unsteady.

"Let me."

Isabeau's hands are gentle as she lays them over mine. She settles my girdle just so, tucks a stray wisp of hair out of sight beneath my wimple. Her touch is familiar, comforting, and all I want is to bolt the door of this room and stay here, in the safety of her arms, until the castle and every man in it turns to dust.

"Thank you." Even my whisper trembles.

"Agnès." Isabeau's brown eyes, the color of doeskin, meet mine with more conviction than I can possibly feel. Her palm is warm where it cups my cheek, and I lean into her, desperate for her touch. "It is not too late to run."

My chest goes tight. We used to dream of leaving this place together. Those first harrowing months, we plotted it all in whispers against each other's skin: the route we would take from this chamber, the supplies we would carry, how we would bind our breasts with linen strips and disguise ourselves as men. But we never made it past the door in truth. Isabeau was willing, but I was afraid. Where would we go, two highborn women alone? I know how to survive Robert, but not the wider woods. We would not be the first women to vanish, only our torn clothing found shredded in the duff as evidence of our fates.

For me, running was only ever a dream. It is the only thing Isabeau and I have ever fought about, and I cannot bear to argue again now.

I shake my head. "We will survive this. We survived him before. His return does not negate our vows."

Those vows, and having Isabeau by my side, were what saw me through the first year in this castle, through everything Robert forced on me before he was called to the holy war. I recall it now, the moment Isabeau and I exchanged our promises: the empty chapel; moonlight silvering the altar; a statue of the Virgin Mary bearing witness, smiling her blessing, as we swore our hearts and loyalty to one another before the eyes of God. When I was escorted back to that same chapel the following morning for my sham of a wedding with Robert, I mouthed the words so that I would not draw attention but did not speak them aloud. My loyalty, and my vows, were meant for Isabeau alone. I knew my Lord in heaven would understand.

We did survive that year before the king called his armies to the Crusade. We survived, but the reminder does not melt my cold fear. I am not as innocent as I was at seventeen; I know what Robert is capable of. I know that survival has its cost.

But it is a cost I can—I must—pay.

I wrap my rosary around my palm and turn to the door.

In Robert's absence, I spent little time in the castle's great hall. There were rarely any guests to entertain, and I never liked how sitting at the head of the table on a raised dais made me feel like another spoil of the hunt put on display. That is exactly how I feel now as I cross the room, the rushes whispering against my skirt's long hem and heads turning to watch my progress.

Robert and his men are already seated, food and ale before them and armor discarded. My hands tighten into fists as I draw near, but I keep my face impassive.

He likes it too much when I am afraid.

A snarl erupts from behind the table as I near its head, and I flinch. Robert has had the hunting dogs brought in from the kennel. A dozen of them squabble over bones, scrabbling through the rushes. I've never liked having the hounds inside—they make me uneasy, all ribs and teeth, kept half starving so they are keen to hunt—but Robert has always relished watching them fight.

Heart beating too fast, I pull my gaze away from the dogs. I sit beside Robert and reach for my chalice. I wish Isabeau were here to give me confidence—but better that she stays away, so that he does not see her and suspect what she means to me.

There was a time I was not made of glass and fractured edges. I was not like this before Robert. I was not like this when he was gone. I ran the keep with confidence in my decisions. I kept its people safe from cold and starvation. I laughed at idle things. I miss myself already, and it has been less than a day.

"The hunting master tells me of a monster."

I blink, jolted from my ruminations.

Robert is watching me. He slouches in his high-backed chair, one hand toying with his eating knife. I know he will not touch me—not here, in front of his men and the servants filling their cups, who all know him as a good and God-fearing man—but danger prickles along my spine.

I am unsurprised that he has already spoken to the hunting master, as there is little Robert loves more than the chase, but he could have learned of the rumors from anyone; it has been at the fore of the entire castle's mind for days. Women have always gone missing from time to time, but since the last full moon, three men have been found dead at the edge of the forest—disemboweled, their entrails strewn across the half frozen earth and hearts torn half eaten from shattered chests. After the second death, I ordered the tenants and their livestock brought inside the castle walls, even though it is not yet full winter. Whatever killed the men seems to have no taste for sheep or kine, since the bodies were discovered ripped open close beside untouched flocks, but I did not wait for it to develop a craving for tenderer flesh.

The manner and number of deaths is unusual, but hardly as cursed as the rumors would have it. It has been a cruel autumn, and the cold makes predators hungry.

"Surely my lord knows better than to listen to idle gossip," I say carefully. "There are no monsters, only wolves and men."

Robert pushes a fatty gobbet of meat around with his knife. Rabbit, I think; there have been no deer hunts since he left, much to my relief. "Wolves that take no animals? That leave no tracks? That kill strong men but leave the herds untouched?"

I lower my eyes to my board so he can find no offense in my gaze. Red juices leak from the meat, sinking into the wood. Of course he did not actually want my thoughts, even though I was the one responsible for the castle's wellbeing—and for handling the killings—while he was gone.

"Then what does my lord think the explanation might be?"

"A punishment, of course."

Confusion makes me look up at him. It is a mistake: his eyes entrap mine, watching for my reaction.

"A punishment? For what?" I ask cautiously—not because I want to, but because he expects it.

"For your sins."

I suck in a startled breath, and the tang of blood and innards assaults my nose. The hounds have torn open a bit of carcass and are fighting over the scraps. Their growls and rumbles cover my husband's words from the rest of the room.

"I know, Agnès." Robert's eyes bore into mine. "I know you have been unfaithful to me."

My bones turn to ice. What passes between Isabeau and me is no sin; we have taken the holiest of vows to one another before the eyes of God. Robert is the one who sins every time he forces his will on me, but he will not see it that way. He will separate Isabeau and me. He will strip her of her station, cast her out into the cold—

"Was it with the master of falcons?" Robert presses. "The cook? A lowly stable boy? I have asked the steward for a list of every man who has visited this castle in my absence. If he was noble, it will not protect him. But if you tell me now, I will consider being merciful."

He does not know. I am uncertain whether to gasp with relief or to sob. He understands nothing; his questions are only paranoia, a gangrenous scar he brought home from the Crusade.

"I have only ever been faithful to my vows," I tell him. I think of Isabeau and manage to hold his gaze. I am telling the truth, and if God disapproved of what I've done, He would have made His will known long ago.

Robert's eyes narrow. "I *will* discover you."

"There is nothing to discover, I swear it." My fist is white around my rosary. "My lord, the steward will confirm that my handmaiden has slept by my side every night these past seven years, guarding my virtue." Sharing my bed is part of her role. No one would—no one *should*—suspect anything different.

Robert's hand tightens on his eating knife. "Then you need a new handmaiden. One who will keep you virtuous."

A void opens in my stomach. He will not—he cannot—

"I will make inquiries," Robert says. "A household must be run with a firm and Godly hand."

His chair screeches as he pushes it back, standing.

"I *will* root out the sin in this household." His hand settles on my shoulder, and I freeze. "I may have failed in the Holy Lands, but I will not fail here."

My tongue is numb, unable to answer even if I thought it would make a difference. He believes he has caught the scent of a quarry, and there is nothing Robert likes better than the hunt.

He raises his voice so the rest of the hall may hear him. "Eat well tonight, but do not drink too well. At dawn we ride out to hunt a monster."

His men cheer, raising their chalices high. Robert smiles, his fingers digging into the meat of my shoulder.

He leans close to my ear. "You too, my lady wife. You will ride with us to face the consequences of your sin."

I pick up my eating knife, but I have no appetite.

All night, I cannot sleep. I toss and turn within the circle of Isabeau's arms, expecting Robert's fist on the door at any moment. Cold sweat prickles my skin as I imagine him coming to take what he believes is his. A lord requires an heir, after all, just as a hunter his game.

"You need to rest," Isabeau says softly.

I turn to face her. I have left a rush light burning—I have been unable to face the darkness since the first night Robert forced himself on me—and its light catches on our unbound hair, my raven interweaving with her bronze on our shared pillow. I trace the contours of her face with reverent fingers: her wide brown eyes, the determined bow of her lips.

She is so brave, my Isabeau, and I wish I could be brave for her, too. If only I could hide my own fears better, be the fortress she deserves against the world. If only I had been brave enough to run with her when she asked. Maybe it would have been possible before Robert returned, but now we would be stopped before we even made it out of the keep. Now there is no escape, only survival.

But how will I survive without Isabeau? If Robert sends her away, what will be worth surviving for?

"I wish we had run." The words are foolish, but I can't stop myself from saying them, a confession never to leave the chapel of our shared bed.

Isabeau doesn't tell me I should have listened to her, because she is kind as well as strong; it is one of the things I've always loved about her. "I wish so, too," she says.

We hold each other tight, until I feel her breathing slow into sleep. But I watch the rush light burn to crumbling ash and do not dare to close my eyes.

It feels like an eternity before dawn stains the sky red. Robert has not come, but that only makes me dread the future more; he is a man whose moods build over time rather than dissipate. When I wake, I find the bed stained too and a deep ache low in my stomach. Spots of blood have soaked through my chemise to speckle the snowy sheets: my cycle, always irregular, has arrived early.

At least I can use it as an excuse to deny Robert if he comes for me tonight. For all his eagerness to spill blood, he is squeamish when it comes from between a woman's legs.

But there is no denying him when it comes to the hunt, even if he may be temporarily repulsed from my bed. Isabeau gathers rags and sends for willow tea, and we help each other dress. We don additional layers to brace for the long cold hours of the hunt, but no brightly colored wool will make me feel warm in my heart.

There has been no hunt proper since before Robert left with the king, and as I step into the castle yard, my senses are assaulted. He has called forth the full force of the chase. The yard churns with saddled horses, tossing their heads against the grooms' reins and stamping as they scent the excitement in the air. Dozens of dogs scrabble at the end of their leather leashes, agitated by the scent of blood and fewmets. A few wives bear short wooden cudgels to bring up the party's rear, their faces a mixture of eagerness and fatigue.

And then, of course, there are the men. Hunting master and kennel master, pages and squires and men-at-arms, groomsmen and trackers and handlers, and Robert's loyal knights who rode with him to the Crusades—that is, those who survived to return.

My stomach wrenches, and I bite down on a grimace. I know better than to ask to stay behind.

A groom assists me onto my horse, a dun palfrey readied with a sidesaddle, the kind that has a rest for my feet and a high pommel to grasp. Unlike the other wives, I will not have my hands free. Cudgels are not for the lady of the castle. One of Robert's men, already mounted on his own destrier, reaches for the reins to lead me. Never mind that I ran the keep in my husband's absence; now that he is returned, everyone seems to have forgotten what I am capable of. Especially me.

Another man hands Isabeau up to her own mount. I would rather she stayed behind—something fierce and animal mantles within me at the idea of Robert looking at her, and besides, hunts can be dangerous—but it would be odd if my handmaiden were not by my side.

The hunting master reviews the plan, addressing the entire assembly, but I barely listen; his voice blends with the groan of the wind around the ramparts. I jolt to attention only when we begin to move. My palfrey and I are carried forward on the flow of a relentless current of bodies, following the dogs barking and straining at their leads. I clench the pommel with hands gone numb within my leather gloves as the portcullis's shadow passes overhead and the castle spits us out.

Snow fell thick during the night, piling on the branches of the trees and mounding in drifts, and it is falling still. Wet flakes sting my cheeks, and the horses' legs sink nearly to the hocks. A horn blows, then another. The hunting master shouts a command. The scenting-hound at the fore of our procession picks up speed as she catches the trail of her quarry. I clutch my cloak tighter around my neck with one hand as the wind knifes along my throat, and bow my head as we ride on and on.

A cacophony of barking rises from the dogs. A horn blows again, and the kennel master releases the first dozen running-hounds, who whip between the dark trees and are gone in a flash.

We must be closing in on our quarry. Truthfully, I do not think there is anything monstrous to find. The dogs must be scenting a deer, or perhaps a boar.

But what if Robert is right? What if there *is* a monster somewhere in the forest?

The thought should not excite me, given that this creature has killed three men, that more than three women have vanished over the years among these trees. But something unfurls in my stomach, something base and hungry, at the notion that Robert and his knights are not the most powerful beings in this wood.

"Hark!" shouts the hunting master. "Forward!"

Now the chase begins in earnest. The riders goad their steeds. The man guiding my palfrey hauls on her reins. We plunge into the forest in a blur of trees and horses, a trampling of vegetation and a showering of snow from the beaten evergreen branches. Ahead of me, Robert in his crimson cloak rides close behind the dogs, boar spear ready to hand. He does not look back as he and his men are swallowed by the woods. He may have said this hunt is for my sake, but he has made his point by dragging me out of the castle. Now it is all for him.

My palfrey struggles against the deepening snow, slower than the rest of the company due to her slighter build. The man holding her reins curses under his breath as he urges her forward, eager to see the hounds run our quarry to bay.

"Go easy," Isabeau tells him sharply. "Can't you see my lady is unwell?"

The man-at-arms gives her a sullen glance, but relents in his efforts. Resentment at missing the chase flows from him like a cold wind.

Cramps pull at my stomach again. I close my eyes for a moment, dizzy, nauseated. The snow is deeper here, and each of my palfrey's strides is a stab through my abdomen. The wind hisses through the branches, equal in loudness now to the baying of the hounds. Horns low, directing the hunters, but even that is grown faint; the main troupe has pulled far ahead, leaving only Isabeau and I, and our minders.

Whatever creature they chase is moving fast, and heading I know not where. I used to know this forest better—Isabeau and I spent time plotting out the routes we might take if we ever fled—but between the thickly falling flakes and my illness, I have entirely lost track of where we are. The procession has left a churn of trampled ground I could follow back to the castle, but I have no other landmark. In every direction, the woods are a blur of black trunks and white snow and—

Red. Between the trees, I catch a glimpse of violent red.

I blink hard against the snow that has caught on my lashes, peering between the trees. A scarlet flash of movement, a wound against the white. A fox? But no, it is too bright, too large, too fast. No fox has ever moved like that, sinuous and so quick my eyes can barely follow.

A crack of branches makes me twist in the saddle, so fast I am nearly unbalanced.

My breath catches in my lungs, and suddenly I have no thoughts of red.

Eyes. Eyes like full moons watch me from between snow-laden evergreen boughs, only a few paces away. A pair level with my head—and then another set appears a little higher up, and then another—

The hounds' cries rise to a frenzy, slashing through the thick air. The eyes vanish. I sit up straighter with a gasp.

"My lady?" Isabeau asks.

I search the trees, but now there are no eyes. No glimpses of red save a few stubborn rose hips clinging to thorny stems. I must be imagining things, dazed by my lack of sleep and the pain of my cycle. I shake my head in response to Isabeau's questioning gaze.

The baying is louder now, nearer. It ululates between the trees, sending a shiver along my nape.

"They've turned," the man-at-arms says. He tugs my palfrey's reins, urging her forward once more. "We can intercept them."

We cut away from the swath of disturbed snow and into the unmarked forest, heading towards the sound of the hunt.

It grows swiftly louder as our horses wade through the snow. The hounds are close, and they are closing in on their quarry. Their baying rings in my ears, punctuated at frequent intervals by the wail of the riders' horns. Now I hear voices, too, the hungry cries of men melding with the dogs'. My palfrey's nostrils flare as she catches a scent too faint for my human nose.

I do not think it is a deer we're hunting.

My hands are bloodless on the pommel, my heart haring madly with both anticipation and fear. I need to see this creature that disembowels men.

The dogs' baying erupts into a cacophony of barking and shouting and snarls. Through it rises the harsh sound of human shouting, but I cannot make out the words—only the tone, raw and unrestrained. I think that is the kennel master, shouting furiously at the pack, but that cannot be right; the dogs have run their quarry to bay, why would he be angry?

Movement teems between the trees ahead, yellow and umber and ultramarine. We have found the hunt. Any moment now Robert will rush in to strike the killing blow with his spear, the archers at the ready should his blade fail. Any moment now, I will see the creature we've been chasing.

As we break through the trees, I realize something is wrong.

Instead of poised to strike the killing blow from horseback, Robert and his men-at-arms are on foot, fighting for control of horses that shy and buck. A knot of hounds is clustered around something on the ground, gulping down mouthfuls of pink fleshy lengths while grooms and pages and men-at-arms alike struggle to drag them away. Red—the dark, purplish red of innards—stains the snow between the dogs' thrashing bodies. A scent-hound breaks free of her handler and dives into the center of the pack to feverishly gobble bits of viscera, heedless of the kennel master's commands and the pages who shout and lunge for her collar.

The knot of men and dogs breaks apart, leaving a gap through which their mangled quarry is visible.

Isabeau presses her knuckles to her mouth. "Agnès, don't look—"

But I have already seen.

Lying in the snow, limbs bent at broken angles and eyes staring blank at the sky, is one of Robert's knights—stomach and ribs flayed open, what innards the dogs have not eaten steaming against the blood-pinked snow.

The hunting party is somber as we return to the castle, speaking little and only in muted voices. They gathered up the dead man as best they could, loose pieces bundled into a cloak that is black with blood by the time we reach the outer walls. Someone must have ridden ahead to tell his wife, for she is waiting at the gate when we arrive, holding two children of around nine or ten by the hand. Her eyes are wide and a bruise yellows her cheek. She is in shock; perhaps that's why she doesn't cry.

Whispers slither through the castle like wind through the trees. *Like no natural animal—led us in circles—as if it knew—*

That evening, Robert comes to my chamber.

I've already removed my wimple and overdress and am preparing for bed, my hair hanging loose to my waist, when the door crashes open so hard it rebounds from the stone wall. The comb clatters from my fingers as I jump to my feet, instinctively reaching for Isabeau.

"This is your doing." Robert's face is dark with the anger he never shows to anyone else, the anger he so carefully conceals behind his mask of piety. He kicks the door closed and is across the room in two strides, driving me from Isabeau as I back away. My shoulders hit the wall, but he does not slow his advance until his feet could crush my toes.

Robert looms over me, his eyes sharp and black. "Your sins created this monster. A good man is dead because of you."

I open my mouth, but he gives me no room to speak.

"How many times?" he demands. "How many men? Did you make a deal with the Devil to keep it hidden from the castle staff?"

I shake my head, my heart slamming against the cage of my ribs. "My lord, I never—"

Robert's hand snakes out to bracket my throat.

"Confess," he hisses. A drop of spittle stings my cheek. "Confess, or I will have it out by force!"

His eyes are bloodshot, his teeth bared. His breath reeks of ale. His thumb digs into the hollow between my collarbones, finding my heartbeat, thready and frantic. Terror renders me mute, unable to speak even if I wished to answer him.

I have always been afraid of the man I was forced to marry, but this is different. Now I barely even recognize him. Earlier, I'd thought he'd returned from the Crusade unchanged, but now I realize that the Holy Lands did transform him—only not in the way I'd hoped. Something has snapped within him, some restraint that used to hold him back from enacting his worst instincts. He is a hound unleashed, and like the hunting dogs he so loves, he will not stop now that he has the scent. Not until something is dead and bloody.

"Tell me!" Robert roars. "Tell me now!"

His hand tightens on my throat. I choke for air, my vision staining red at the edges. My hands rise to scrabble at his fingers, but he is too strong for me. He will kill me, I cannot breathe—

Suddenly Robert falls back, releasing me. I retch, my hands going to my bruised throat. Robert spits a curse, and—oh God, Isabeau. My brave, determined Isabeau. She has thrown herself on him, her thin arms hooked around his neck from behind as she tries to drag him away from me.

With a guttural sound, Robert throws Isabeau off. She stumbles into the bed frame, loses her balance, tumbles to hands and knees. He strides towards her, face twisted with rage.

A white-hot desperation burns through my fear. I will not let him touch her: my Isabeau, my heart, my everything.

With a strength I did not know I possessed, I rush at Robert and shove him with all my might.

His eyes widen, and then he is falling, his foot skidding out from beneath him. His arms flail but meet only air as he topples backwards and his head strikes the wall.

The crack of his skull meeting stone—I feel it somewhere deep and visceral.

Silence rings through the chamber. My chest heaving, I stare down at Robert, sprawled in a motionless heap. Blood seeps along the floorboards from the back of his head. For a wondering, terrible moment I think I have killed him.

Then his chest rises, and he groans. My stomach clenches. I should be relieved that I have not stained my hands with murder, but instead exhaustion drags low in my gut like menstrual cramps. Will we never be free of him?

"Agnès," Isabeau gasps, pushing herself to her feet. Her hands cup my face. "Are you—"

Unharmed—she is unharmed. That is all that matters. I kiss her, desperate and fierce, until a groan from Robert forces me to break away. There is no time to waste.

"He will not forgive this." My voice is raw, the print of Robert's hand seared into my throat, but I ignore the pain. "You must run now, I will keep him distracted—"

"No." Isabeau's hands tighten on mine. "Never. Not without you."

I wind my fingers through hers, each knuckle bone a bead on our shared rosary. I do not know whether it is courage at last or merely desperation, but I make my choice. "Then we must go. Now."

There is no time to pack, no time to prepare. Robert is stirring, and once he wakes it will be too late. We drag on our overdresses and snatch up a pair of cloaks, and we hurry from the room.

Hand in hand, we rush through the back corridors of the keep, past startled servants whose eyes widen at the sight of us, disheveled and bruised with our hair shockingly uncovered. Down the passages we mapped out all those years ago when we dreamed of running but I never dared. Out of the keep, across the yard, and through the hidden postern gate behind the castle stables.

We force the gate open past frozen hinges and are outside the castle walls, out into the winter dark. The night is bitter, snow still falling thick and dense. Cold seeps through my thin leather shoes and bites my ankles as each step sinks calf-deep into the drifts, and I gasp as an icy wind whips down the neck of my cloak.

We will not survive the cold for long. And the cold is far from the only danger. I think of full moon eyes and twisted innards and shreds of cloth half buried among the roots, of vanished women and dark blood steaming in the snow.

But we will not survive Robert either, not this time. I would rather take my chances with the woods.

I grasp Isabeau's hand and we run for the trees. Branches close their arms around us and the wind quiets from a scream to a lilting sigh, as if the woods are breathing. The tell-tale mouths of our tracks gape behind us, but if we can gain enough distance before a search party is mounted, the falling snow will cover our path, bury our scent.

A bell begins to toll. And then, keening louder than the wind in the treetops: the baying of hounds.

My heart seizes, and my hand tightens on Isabeau's. I feel Robert's hand around my throat again, making each breath a struggle.

We are quarry, and there is nothing my husband and his dogs love better.

"Agnès," Isabeau urges. I have stopped moving without realizing it, pinned beneath the memory of my husband.

I shake off my paralysis and pull her forward with me. There is no time for fear. No time for anything but this one last chance at survival, or something more. The snow will not help us now; only speed can save us. We break into a run, as fast as we can force our legs through the deep drifts.

Wind howls; the dogs cry. I do not dare look back, only to run, to run, to run. My chest is full of knives and Isabeau gasps for breath, but we cannot stop, cannot look back. Some part of me understands our flight is useless, that we do not stand a chance—two women on foot against a full hunting party and their scent-hounds, not to mention whatever creature tore that man apart. But the brand of Robert's fingers burns my throat, and the sight of Isabeau thrown to the ground is seared into my eyes, and so I grit my teeth against the cold, stumble forward on feet gone numb. For Isabeau I would run until my legs are worn to stubs, until the winter's teeth have stripped all the skin from my body.

I am so cold now I no longer feel the pain, only the press of my lover's hand in mine. The hounds' cries surround us, and movement flashes through the trees. They have found us now. Our flight is all for naught. Lithe bodies weave through the trees on all sides, glowing red as carmine against the wet-black trees and blanching snow—

And I gasp, for no hound in Robert's kennels is that shade of red.

Keeping pace with our race through the storm are sinuous four-legged creatures with scales like rubies and eyes like moons. The same eyes I saw watching me on the hunt. There must be dozens of them, but not a one gives chase; no, they are running *with* us, as if Isabeau and I with our stumbling human legs are a part of their graceful pack.

Sisters, the creatures whisper, a caress against my mind. *At last.*

And suddenly, though the snow is still deep and the night still fierce, I am no longer tired. My pain is gone, my breaths easy and deep. I grasp Isabeau's hand and I run, I run, I run, but I am no longer the quarry fleeing the hunters; I revel in my speed, I am made for giving chase. My legs grow lithe and strong. My hands sprout claws and reach for the earth, carrying me along so easy and fleet on four powerful limbs. My cloak and dress slough away, no longer needed, and beneath them the cold has dyed my skin a rich and vibrant red.

I look to Isabeau, running beside me, and when we smile at one another her teeth are as long and sharp as mine.

Part of the pack, we scream our freedom to the winter skies.

And then, with our sisters, we turn towards the hounds and the foolish men who follow, men whose hearts will taste so sweet and just.

The hunt begins.

LA MALDIT-COMIAT

BRIANA MORGAN

THE FLUTTERY KICK CAME low in Chrysanta's belly, a distinct, butterfly ripple against the rigid busk of her corset, and she knew, with the terrifying certainty of a woman whose body was no longer entirely her own, that she was with child.

She eyed the wooden bucket of vomit sitting in the corner. The acrid scent of bile mingled with the drying lavender hanging in bunches from the rafters, creating a cloying atmosphere that clung to the back of her throat. It was only a matter of time before this happened. Gaubert hadn't been careful—but then, carelessness was the singular privilege of a Duke's son. It was a luxury he wore as easily as his velvet doublets.

Chrysanta shifted on the straw mattress. Her bed still smelled of his hair oil—sandalwood and expensive musk—and the salt of his sweat. The scent, once intoxicating, once a promise of intimacy and warmth against the Gascony chill, now turned her stomach. She would need a great deal of money to make everything go away. She wanted to get back to singing, back to the dusty road, back to a life that belonged to her.

Gaubert would never marry her. That much she knew. As the heir to the Duchy of Gascony, he had higher marriage aspirations than a wandering troubairitz with calloused fingers and road-worn hems. He needed land, titles, and political alliances. She only offered songs.

As she reflected on their clandestine trysts—the stolen moments in haylofts where the dust motes danced in shafts of golden light, the evenings by the riverbanks where the water kissed the stones—she wondered if she'd made the right decisions. In the beginning, they'd had fun. He'd made her happier, feel more alive, than anyone else ever had. He had looked at her as if she were the sun, and she, starving for warmth, had let herself be burned.

Then, she'd quickened, and he had vanished.

Chrysanta pressed a hand against her stomach, her palm seeking the life growing there. Her dresses were already tightening at the waist. Before long, she would be harboring a bastard child with no patron to protect them. She could contact Gaubert, certainly. She could arrange to meet with him and beg, kneeling in the dirt, but what would that get her? Marked as difficult. Exiled. Banished to the woods to birth the babe on a bed of damp moss, where the winter wolves would likely take them both.

She should leave Gascony. She should pack her lute, wrap her few belongings in oilcloth, and seek a life somewhere new. Perhaps she could trick a merchant into a quick marriage to hide her indiscretion—find a widower with poor eyesight and a need for a mother to his brood. It wasn't as if she didn't know the road. She had been drifting from town to town for years before settling here, surviving on coin tossed into her instrument case and the kindness of strangers.

But Lord Gaubert would go nowhere. He would remain unaffected by their shared sin, stepping out into society with his reputation burnished by a bit of sowing wild oats. Society would neither condemn him nor ostracize him. For that, Chrysanta envied him as much as she hated him—which, as it turned out, was quite a great deal.

Once this baby was born, she would teach it to hate him, too.

Chrysanta stood, her knees cracking in the damp morning air, and grabbed her lute. The wood was smooth and cool under her touch, a familiar friend. She idly plucked the gut strings, listening to the resonance fade into the silence of the cottage. The remnants of *le maldit-comiat*—a song of cursing and farewell—floated across her troubled mind. Her fingers rushed to their orders.

She had to be ready.

When the Duke showed up on Chrysanta's doorstep two days later, the sound of his entourage shattered the peace of the morning. Hooves clattered on the hard-packed earth, and the jingle of bridles announced wealth arriving where it did not belong.

It was all she could do not to slam the oak door in his face. Instead, she offered him a curtsy and wished him well.

Womanhood was swallowing pain with a smile. It was a lesson she had learned young, and one she practiced daily.

Duke Emil of Gascony was not an old man, though he carried the weight of his title like a heavy, suffocating cloak. His beard was peppered with gray, and his eyes were the color of flint. Chrysanta had seen him several times, but only ever at a distance, usually from the back of a crowd while she performed, or riding past on a high horse while she walked in the mud.

How did he know where she lived? The thought sent a spike of ice down her spine.

Emil de Gascony smiled, but the expression did not reach his eyes. It was a muscular contraction, nothing more. "Chrysanta, I presume?"

"Yes, My Lord." Chrysanta made to drop into a deeper curtsy, keeping her eyes on his polished boots, which were already gathering dust from her floor.

Emil waved her off. "No need," he said, his voice dry as parchment. "We will soon be past that."

It was an ominous preamble. Emil asked her to invite him in. She would rather have choked down a live eel, but she opened the door wide, because men like Emil could not tell the lies they wanted to believe from the truth standing before them. And because refusing a Duke was a good way to have one's house burned down.

When she offered him a seat, the Duke didn't sit. He stood with his hands in his pockets, silently appraising everything she owned—the chipped washbasin, the single tallow candle burned down to a nub, the drying herbs that failed to mask the scent of poverty. He was calculating the worth of her life and finding it lacking.

"I have heard... rumors," Emil began, turning his gaze to her. "It has been hard to ignore them. Rumors about you and my son, Lord Gaubert."

Chrysanta wanted to crawl beneath the earth and fade away to nothing. She knew little of what constituted a "problem" to Emil, but considering he'd made the time to visit her personally, leaving his estate to stand in a peasant's hovel, the situation was dire.

"What sort of rumors, Your Grace?" Chrysanta asked, forcing her voice to remain steady, tucking her trembling hands into the folds of her skirt.

"About your lack of chastity," he said, the words dripping with disdain. "Your predation upon his youth. Your indiscretion."

Chrysanta felt the blood drain from her face. This was the visit she'd been dreading since she first kissed Gaubert last summer under the willow tree.

"Is it true?" Emil asked.

"We have been...together." Chrysanta wrung her hands, playing the part of the nervous, heartbroken lover. She let a wobble enter her voice. "And I love him, Your Grace. Quite desperately. I believe he loves me, too."

Loved her, maybe. Before. They had spoken at length about their shared future. Long before the baby, they'd wanted children. They wanted to live in Gascony in the same house, the one he had grown up in. Although marriage was impossible given his status, he'd said it was all he wanted. A union with Chrysanta.

She'd been so naive. She could tell the Duke thought so, too. He looked at her not with pity, but with the annoyance one might feel for a fly buzzing near their wine.

Emil's eyebrows shot up. He cleared his throat, looking as if he had swallowed something sour. "I admit, I was not expecting such a confession. Rather...this makes the circumstances of my visit much more difficult." He swallowed. "You see, I have come to hire you to play and sing at my son's wedding."

The air left the room. The silence that followed was heavy, ringing in Chrysanta's ears. It felt like she stood at the edge of a precipice and Emil had nudged her off balance.

"His wedding?" Chrysanta whispered. The word felt like a curse.

"Yes. In three days."

He wanted her to perform for them. He wanted the whore to sing for the virgin bride. He wanted to parade his son's conquest in front of the court, to show that the overarching power of the Duchy could bend even heartbreak to its will.

Chrysanta fought the urge to be sick. She looked at the floor, letting the silence stretch, letting him think he had broken her.

"I couldn't," she said softly. "I cannot watch him pledge himself to another."

"You can, and you will," Emil said, reaching into his doublet and tossing a heavy leather purse onto her small table. The coins clinked—a heavy, decisive sound that echoed off the wooden walls. "That is enough to see you out of Gascony and set you up comfortably in the north. You will play, you will humiliate yourself by showing you are nothing to him, and then you will vanish."

Chrysanta stared at the purse. It was bulging. It was more money than she had made in five years of touring. It was enough for the baby. Enough for a new life. Enough to buy silence.

"Who is she?" Chrysanta asked. "The bride?"

She shouldn't ask. She knew she shouldn't ask. Yet she had to hear him say it.

"Lady Isolde of Leona," Emil said.

Chrysanta's face went slack. Her heart slowed to the point she felt like it had stopped beating. Playing at the party meant...what? Being set up for the rest of her life? Providing for her child and its uncertain future?

Or inescapable heartbreak?

And there, in the back of her mind, hung the question of what *Gaubert* wanted. Was this wedding his idea? Did he *love* his bride-to-be?

Chrysanta battled memories of Gaubert, happier times, and all the promises he'd made her. Every glimpse into the past pricked her like a needle. But Emil was a reminder of the pain, and the money was her escape from it.

"I shall play," she answered, her voice hollow.

Emil's mouth twitched. "Excellent."

He turned and left without another word, the door swinging shut behind him, leaving the scent of expensive leather and cruelty in his wake.

The day of the wedding dawned hot and oppressive. The heat in Gascony was a physical weight, rising from the vineyards in shimmering waves.

The Duke's estate loomed like a fortress on the horizon, a sprawling mass of gray stone jutting out from the rolling hills. It was a display of power, designed to make anyone approaching feel small. As Chrysanta walked the long, dust-choked road toward the gates, her lute strapped to her back, she felt the eyes of the stone gargoyles watching her.

The courtyard was a chaotic sea of activity. Servants rushed past with platters of roasted pheasant, their feathers reattached for display, and jugs of spiced wine that sweat in the heat. The air smelled of roasting meat—whole boars turning on spits, fat dripping into the fires with a hiss—mingled with heavy perfumes, horse manure, and the underlying, metallic tang of greed.

She was led to the Great Hall, a cavernous room draped in tapestries of crimson and gold depicting hunts and battles. The sheer volume of noise was staggering. A hundred aristocrats, already drunk on the Duke's best vintage, shouted and laughed, their voices bouncing off the vaulted stone ceiling.

Chrysanta took her place on a small wooden stage at the front of the room, balancing the lute on her thighs. The wood felt slippery in her sweating hands. The songs she'd chosen wouldn't suit the occasion, but they would suit her performance.

This crowd would be easy to please. They were already drunk on excess. They tore at bread with greasy fingers and spilled wine down their silken fronts. After so many years of performing, she could smell it on the wind when a success loomed close at hand. The most significant factor in an artist's success is confidence in her abilities. The second is the ability to control the room.

Still, she did not see Gaubert. She was grateful for this small blessing. Although she had taken this job as what was best for her family, she felt the sludge of trepidation sliding down her back. It would be painful seeing him, not only after what happened, but with someone else.

The baby stirred inside of her, a restless tumble, as if sensing her adrenaline. She quelled the urge to place a hand on her stomach to comfort the child. She wouldn't start a scandal here. She wouldn't endanger the plan.

Suddenly, the trumpets blared, a brassy shriek that cut through the din.

Tousled chestnut hair flashed scarlet in the sunlight streaming through the high windows as Gaubert stepped into view. He looked every bit the pampered noble, handsome and vacant, waving to the crowd who cheered his name. And there, on his arm...

Isolde.

Her hair was burnished gold, a halo caught in the candlelight. She wore white silk embroidered with pearls, a vision of purity that made Chrysanta's breath hitch. She moved with a grace that made the heavy fabric seem like water. Heat bloomed in Chrysanta's chest, blood rising in her cheeks.

Easy, she reminded herself. *You must make it through this.*

She remembered meeting Gaubert at the harvest festival, how he had charmed her with a stolen apple and a crooked smile. But her mind betrayed her, slipping past him to the moment she met Isolde, months later, in the shadowy corner of the chapel where Chrysanta had gone to pray for guidance. Isolde had been crying, her face hidden in her hands. They had spoken for hours, whispering in the dark until the candles burned low.

Seeing the two of them there, hand in hand, stung Chrysanta's heart so hard it nearly stopped beating. But not for Gaubert. Never for Gaubert.

If she told him about the child, perhaps he would surprise her. Perhaps he wouldn't turn his head, deny his love, call her a whore like many others would. Perhaps he would even grow to love the child.

But then, she'd always been a dreamer with her head in the clouds.

Chrysanta grabbed her lute and strummed a jarring, dissonant chord that cut through the chatter of the crowd. The guests turned, startled, grease shining on their chins.

This song must be perfect. She must be perfect.

She played the opening notes of a melody Gaubert would recognize. It was the same song she sang for him after their first time together, when his eyelids were thick with sleep and lips hot with unkept promises.

Gaubert froze. He looked toward the stage, his eyes widening as he recognized her. Panic flared in his gaze. He looked quickly to his father, then to his bride, terror written in the set of his jaw.

Chrysanta's gaze drifted to Isolde. The bride was not looking at her groom. She was looking at the stage. Isolde's face was unreadable to the court—a mask of porcelain perfection—but to Chrysanta, it was a map of shared secrets. A slight narrowing of the eyes. A twitch of a finger against the tablecloth.

Chrysanta's fingers danced over the strings, the music flowing like water in a stream.

Le maldit-comiat.

It was a genre of song typically used by a man to condemn a female lover, to shame her for her infidelity. But it would suffice. Chrysanta took a sonnet she wrote for Gaubert and twisted the words, sharpening them into daggers. She sang of a love that rots from the inside, of a noble house built on lies, of a wolf in sheep's clothing.

"You swore on the stars," she sang, her voice rising to the rafters, clear and cutting, *"but the stars cannot see the mud in which you crawl."*

A murmur went through the crowd. This was not a wedding song. This was an accusation.

Duke Emil stood up, his face turning a violent shade of purple, a vein throbbing in his temple. "Enough!"

Chrysanta did not stop. She played harder, the music becoming a frenzy, her fingers flying until they ached.

"You have greatly misunderstood your significance here!" the Duke bellowed, his voice booming over the music. "You have made a disgrace of me! Of my son!" He spat on the floor. "You whore."

Chrysanta let the final chord ring out, vibrating in the stunned silence of the hall. She stood, clutching the neck of her lute like a weapon. Shame fell on her like a blanket, but she resisted its touch. She'd fought so hard already.

"Everyone!" the Duke shouted, turning to the confused guests. "This woman is a parasite, a liar, and a whore! She has ruined my son's wedding and does not deserve any further patronage. In fact, I shall do everything in my power to ensure that she is exiled from Gascony!"

A hush fell over the banquet hall. No one had been exiled from Gascony for as long as anyone could remember. Even then, it was because the man committed murder.

"Guards!" Emil screamed. "Seize her!"

Two guards in the Duke's livery stepped forward, their hands reaching for their swords. Chrysanta did not move. She watched the Duke.

Emil took a breath to shout again, but the sound died in his throat. He blinked, confusion replacing the rage on his face. He reached for the table to steady himself, but his hand missed the wood. He swayed, his legs suddenly rubber.

"Father?" Gaubert stood, looking concerned. "Father, what is—"

Gaubert cut off with a wet choke. He grabbed his own throat, his eyes bulging.

At the tables, the scene descended into madness. A Duchess slumped face-first into her roast duck, the sauce splashing onto her neighbor. A Baron slid out of his chair, clawing at the tablecloth, pulling silver goblets down with him in a clatter of metal.

It wasn't instant. It was a slow, terrifying cascade. One by one, the guests began to twitch, to gasp for air that wouldn't come. Hemlock is a cruel mistress; it starts at the feet and works its way up, numbing the body until the lungs simply forget how to breathe.

Chrysanta stood on the stage, watching the chaos unfold with a terrifying calmness. She felt it in her soul—the moment the balance shifted.

The Duke fell to his knees, frothing at the mouth. He looked up at Chrysanta, his eyes wide with realization, before he collapsed to the rushes, dead.

Gaubert was on the floor, gray and bloodless, his tongue lolling from his mouth. He looked toward Isolde, pleading for help, his hand reaching out to grab the hem of her dress.

But Isolde was not helping him. She pulled her skirts away from his grasping fingers with a look of mild distaste.

Isolde sat perfectly still at the head table, her hands folded in her lap. She had not touched the wine. She watched Gaubert die with the detachment of a statue.

Chrysanta, meanwhile, lost a large chunk of her soul as Gaubert's had left his body. Maybe he didn't deserve her grief, but she couldn't help giving him some.

When the last of the death rattles faded, silence reclaimed the hall. It was a heavy, suffocating silence, broken only by the crackle of the hearth fire and the settling of dust.

Chrysanta stepped off the stage. She walked through the carnage, careful not to step on the velvet trains of the dead or the puddles of spilled wine that looked so much like blood. She walked straight to the high table.

"It is done," Chrysanta said.

Isolde looked up. A slow smile spread across her face, radiant and terrible.

"It's hemlock," Isolde said, her voice steady. "I put it in the casks myself. I am glad you did not drink it."

"I was not offered any."

The women exchanged smiles. For the first time in months, Chrysanta felt the knot of anxiety in her chest loosen.

Chrysanta slid her hand into Isolde's and interlaced their fingers. It felt as perfect as it always did, warm and grounding amidst the horror. She knew she'd made the right decision.

Isolde had known about the baby since the start.

The first time they lay together, months ago, Isolde had asked Chrysanta about it. It took a woman to notice the early changes in another woman's body, the way her breasts filled in and her stomach slightly rounded. Isolde had stroked Chrysanta's side and asked her what had happened. Chrysanta told her all about Gaubert, and Isolde had lain there, listening, her anger burning hotter than Chrysanta's own.

"I would never leave you," Isolde had whispered in the dark. It was the best thing Chrysanta had ever heard.

In the present, Chrysanta took Isolde's hand and squeezed it. "I cannot give you the extravagant life you are used to, that he would have given you had you not met me. But I would like to try."

Isolde stood, stepping over the body of the man she was meant to marry. "I do not want an extravagant life, Chrysanta. I have had that life, and would have had it every day hereafter. I want a life that is *ours*."

It would not be easy for them. Their situation was complicated by Isolde's higher station. Although she had some wealth, it would run out. She could not get more without asking her family. If Isolde petitioned them for anything after this tragedy, they might come after their daughter. Chrysanta and Isolde must be ready.

The women held each other. Isolde's arms encircled Chrysanta's waist, pressing against the small bump of the child between them. At that moment, it was as if the wedding never happened.

Chrysanta retrieved her lute, slinging it over her shoulder. The chaos had passed. Now, there was only the work of leaving.

The two of them picked their way through the fallen bodies of the guests.

"We will be a family now," Chrysanta whispered.

"To me, we always have been."

Chrysanta and Isolde had been planning this for months. Having met after Isolde was engaged to Gaubert, they'd discussed how Isolde could get out of her marriage, as she was not interested in men. Chrysanta had confided in her about Gaubert's infidelity, and while it could not be proven, Isolde saw it as the ideal motive for revenge. The pregnancy had only escalated their scheming. Isolde wanted to raise Chrysanta's baby, make them a true family. As desperate as they were to be together, Isolde had been the one to make Chrysanta wait, to perform at the wedding. They needed the Duke's gold. They needed the cover of the feast.

The fact that Chrysanta carried Gaubert's child did not hurt them. It was justice. They would take his bloodline, his gold, and his bride, and raise them all far away from his rot.

Isolde and Chrysanta walked out of the Great Hall, leaving the tomb behind them.

Outside, the sun had set. The air was cool and sweet, a sharp contrast to the charnel house they had left behind. A low, thin mist rolled over the hills and fields of Gascony. It swirled around their ankles like a hungry, dying lover—so eager for connection.

They would wander until they came upon another village in a land that hadn't even heard of Gascony. They'd have each other, and the baby, and they would all be happy.

She would raise her child, boy or girl, not to swallow their pain like she had. She would teach them that sometimes, the only way to build a new world is to burn down the old one.

There Will Be Weeping and Gnashing of Teeth

Amanda Havill Adgate

T HE DIVINE IS HERE. A presence among us, He is a hand on our shoulders, guiding our steps. If I close my eyes, I can sense Him drawing me near, beckoning me closer to sit at His feet. Desire rises in my belly, the need quavering in my bones.

Yes, King, we come. We obey.

The wind pulls at my cloak; the heavy fabric keeps the worst of the chill away from my skin. We walk, a huddled mass of worn brown robes over emaciated frames. I've lost count of the number of steps I've taken, the number of days we've journeyed, moving from town to town in search of sustenance, a place to lay our heads. Our numbers swell as we trek towards the mountains, the seasons changing around us. First it was boiling hot, the grass scalded by the sun. Brown crops curling in the heat. No food anywhere. And now the wind is fierce, nipping at the thin skin holding our bones together. Fatigue claws at us, slows our steps, the hum of many voices our constant companion.

That, and the hunger.

The famine began so long ago, the gnawing ache growing with each passing day, with each rationed morsel. My family's stock of provisions dwindled quickly; too many mouths to feed. It wasn't long before the number of mouths decreased.

When given a choice, I left home and joined the brethren that plod along the dirt path around me. Gave up my family. Lopped off the long auburn locks I was born with.

The Divine had a plan for me, one in which I shall prosper.

Our ragged forms clash with the surrounding glory—the green grass ripples, each blade waving as if to welcome the day. The mountains crowd in close, rising majestically to embrace the bluest sky I've ever seen. This mission has granted me some of the most spectacular sights. Things I never dreamed of seeing.

Doing things I never imagined possible.

"It's The Divine, showing us the way," Elder says, his voice loud enough to reach my ears, even at the back of the procession. The murmurs from my brethren grow stronger, like the buzz of many bees. I remember in a sudden flash the small hive my parents kept, years ago now; the way the tiny creatures droned from flower to flower, covering themselves in sticky orange pollen.

So much has changed since those simple days.

I yank myself from the memory, focusing instead on keeping my breaths even, on echoing the sounds my brethren make, on the moment and not the events surrounding me. *I am a servant, humble and obedient.* There are rules that must be followed. There is a task at hand, and I have seen His majesty, been saved by His mercy. I want to bring glory to The Divine, to obey, to follow without questioning.

Sometimes doubt creeps in, then the guilt. But I've grown familiar with brushing it aside, pulling the doubt free like one would exorcise a weed from a garden.

It is my duty to serve The Divine. I may not understand the call, but I will answer it.

Hunger consumes me, sharp as a blade slicing my skin, but we keep moving forward. Always moving onward, to the next town, the next glade, the next farmhouse. I glance up to see Elder speaking to a scout, the two off to the side of the dusty roadway. We pause as one in our steps, and it takes everything in me not to shift my weight. I am invisible here, and I intend to stay that way. Being noticed invites discord; the best servant is silent, accommodating. Dutiful. Obedient.

The scout points towards the ridge ahead, and I watch Elder nod and raise his hands towards the sky. He turns to us, a pleased smile twisting his lips. Something in my chest stirs—a rattling of bones, a quickening of slowly desiccating heartstrings. I ignore it.

Elder's voice echoes in the stillness. Brash and commanding, the certainty there soothes my nerves. "The Divine is with us, even now, amid our trials. The end is not near, my brothers and sisters. We are following His path, clearing His way to returning. This is but a test, one we will accomplish to His glory. Our next stop has been ordained—our way is clear."

Around me, hands rise, and I quickly join in. *Invisible.* I like it best that way. It is safe.

"Glory and praise to thee." Every mouth recites the common phrase, my voice lost among the echoing call. Cold sweat slides down my spine, and I suppress a shiver, ducking my head as we walk once more. I'm not sure how much time passes, in fits and starts as the last of my strength wanes. My belly cramps; it's been empty too long since I've eaten or rested in the shade of an elm's branches. I nearly weep as a small village comes into view, one thatched roof at a time. With each step, nausea rises in my belly, a vinegar swill that threatens to expel itself from between my clenched teeth.

I want nothing more than to obey. I struggle with sin, with my own selfish feelings, hoping no one notices my internal grappling. Desperate for my doubt to be undetectable. Was this endless journey to find food and share the news of The Divine where I am meant to be? I shake the doubt free, imagining each evil thought like a rotten apple falling from the branches. It won't contaminate the good fruit left behind. I won't let it.

Your will be done, King.

The walk to the village is peaceful. There's no one on the road but us, shuffling lines of brown cloaks, shaved heads hidden from the sunlight under the coarse fabric. The surrounding air warms up insidiously, and I can almost ignore the sweat beginning to tickle my forehead. My hands stay down at my sides; nothing will distract me from my purpose. The rattling of the ox-cart behind me grows louder as it brings up the rear, clattering along, the beast panting from the uphill climb. The beast's taut flesh hangs from the sharp edges of its bones, sweat glistening along its protruding spine. We are all half-starved creatures now.

Villagers appear, their faces open and curious. I can imagine how Elder looks, leading a multitude of cloaked monks into the village proper. The benign smile on his face, the shining benevolence in his eyes. Harmless, holy. *God-touched.* I dare not look up from my soiled feet to take in any of the villagers' faces. It would do no good. Better to stay as unattached as possible. I know what comes next.

Elder continues on, greeting those we pass by, the surrounding brethren still mumbling along, a slow song of words none of these townsfolk will understand—but they will be spellbound. Enchanted.

My belly roils again, from nerves or hunger or a sickening combination of both.

"Greetings to you!" Elder's voice rises into the azure sky, and we all stop, our feet still, our breathing in sync. The brethren are one, united with the sole purpose of serving The Divine as He instructs. The strap of the pack digs into my shoulder, but I dare not move.

The Elder continues speaking, his voice a soothing cadence. "We are but humble travelers, looking for a place to rest for the night. Might you have stables, or know of a field nearby where we can drink and eat for a few moments in peace?"

Another voice responds. "Of course, Father. We are a small town, but won't turn down holy men. It would be an honor to host you this evening."

"May The Divine bless you, sir." Elder turns to face us, spreading his arms wide. "Here we are, devotees, a place to repose before we continue on our journey. What a gift, what a holy appointment we've arrived in time for." His smile grows, glittering in the bright sunshine.

"What brings you here? Visitors are scarce in these parts." Another man steps forward; by the looks of him a simple farmer. Hardworking, God-fearing. I quickly scan the faces around me, taking in the calloused hands, the simple clothes. Honest people.

Yes. *Worthy* people. The Divine is gracious in His gifting. He knows better than I.

"The Great Famine called us from our home. We lost our monastery, and have been wandering these last months, looking for a new place to settle down. Collecting lost souls along the way to add to our ranks." The people around us murmur in sympathy. I can see the pity in their eyes, the softening of their hearts. Something slithers along the edges of my mind, smooth as a river rock, but I brush it away with an idle flick. I am one of the brethren. I have no thoughts of my own.

"Ah. We've heard rumors of the hardships, but were mostly spared." The man who speaks wears the cleanest clothes, ones that haven't needed mending yet. *He must be the one in charge here.* Elder notices as well, for he moves closer to the man, movements sleek and disarming.

Spared. I hardly know the meaning of the word. Hardship after hardship, each taking its pound of flesh, has been the story of my life. Envy slithers through me, pooling in my guts like a sickness before I can shrug the feeling off. I lift my gaze to take in the surrounding folk once more. Their worn clothes, scuffed boots. Sun-kissed cheeks. Not an easy life, but one better than what I've known. Their forms are fed, vivacious in their aliveness. My stomach growls at the thought of food. Perhaps this is the place we've been searching for.

This world is the King's playground—His ways are beyond us.

"The Divine has a purpose for you—perhaps this very moment is the reason you were spared." Elder spreads his arms wide, the hood of his cloak falling back. Sweat gleams on the pale skin of his bald head, liver spots clear from where I'm standing. He is growing older, feebler. The Divine uses him, wielding Elder as a mighty weapon against the evil forces infecting this earth.

And it *is* an infestation. The months of wandering through towns and villages, seeing with my own eyes the horror of this world, revealed how far the rot has spread.

But a new day has come.

Elder continues speaking to the town's leader as the rest of us stand, still as stone pillars. My feet ache from the trek, and all I want to do is lie down in the soft grass and let my eyes close.

Purpose before pleasure. Elder's words fill my mind. It does me no good to give in to the evil one's temptations. After we complete our task, fulfill The Divine's calling, we will be free to pursue leisure.

The town leader brings us to an enormous structure in the center of the village. Sturdy wooden columns hold up its thatched roof, and a layer of sweet-smelling straw covers the cool and dry ground in the shade. My chest heaves, a sob clenched behind my teeth at the welcome sight.

"Thank you for your kindness," Elder speaks for us all, bending his thin body at the waist in a bow. "We've been to many towns these past months, and have experienced little in the way of hospitality." He pauses, tapping a finger to his wizened chin. "We must repay you in some way—but we have no coin. We are humble beings, serving Our King....but perhaps we can offer you freedom from the darkness—teachings from The Divine. It is of the utmost importance, and if you're as secluded as you say, then surely your townsfolk could use a well-said passage of scripture."

The man's eyes widen as a crooked smile stretches across his face. "That would be most welcome, Father. We see little in the way of entertainment nor visitors, like I said. Most of the time we are completely isolated from the outside world. I'm sure everyone would enjoy that."

Elder nods, straightens. "An after-dinner homily, then."

The townsfolk linger at the edge of the structure, watching us with curiosity as we sit down, resting our weary limbs. My shoulders scream in relief as I swing my pack to the dirt, rolling the abused muscles, searching for a way to lessen the tension lingering there. Nothing is helping, and the stress seems to coil tighter, sinking into my bones like a sickness. I lean back against one post, silently praying for healing as my ears discern a hushed conversation nearby. Two brethren are whispering to Elder, and I watch him nod along, listening intently. The remaining ox grazes nearby, greedily ripping thick patches of grass from the earth in sharp movements. I can still recall the taste of his brother, the leathery feel of the meat against my tongue as my teeth tore into the slight portion allotted to me. His tail flicks a fly off his hindquarters, and I jerk my attention back to Elder as he lets out a gentle laugh.

"His ways are unknown to us, Brother Aspertine. I realized when we first arrived that I saw glimpses of this place whenever I closed my eyes during our journey. The town square, the main street leading towards the village…The Divine provides, and we give thanks." His eyes meet mine, and I quickly flinch away, hoping to stay invisible. It would not do to draw Elder's notice. I have seen him do many things in the name of The Divine. The man intimidates me.

The meal the townsfolk provide surprises me. The meat is tender; the potatoes and carrots warm. I inhale half my bowl before thinking to dip the bread in the juices pooling around the vegetables. This is more food than I've eaten in days, and I blink back tears. Of gratitude, of guilt.

Thank you, King. Your ways are just and perfect, even if I can't always see. Forgive me for my doubt. Help me be stronger in You.

A woman hands me a rough-hewn cup, her fingers brushing mine innocently. I nod my thanks, keeping my head bowed. The scent of rosemary and something bitter floats on the breeze. I take a large swig of ale before turning back to the stew left in my bowl. The surrounding brethren are silent, the only sounds the scrape of spoons against the wooden bowls, the light steps of the women wandering between our ranks with jugs of drink. The kindness of these strangers fills my limbs with a weariness that pulls at me. I try to shrug the feeling off, but it remains, a leech on my back where I cannot reach.

Time passes too quickly; Elder stands, moving to address the townspeople who gather at the edge of the structure. "We appreciate beyond words your kindness to us." His words echo off the buildings, and he beckons them closer. As one, those around me stand, and I struggle to keep up. Elder's voice weaves through the crowd, sonorous and soothing. "Come, gentle citizens, come and hear of The Divine and his gracious plan for our lives."

We say nothing as they file into the structure in the center of town, chattering excitedly at the prospect of Elder's soliloquy. The stew sits heavy in the pit of my stomach, less appetizing now that the time has come. My doubt is always strongest just before Elder speaks, knowing what comes after.

But evil dresses as a sheep, tricking the sinner into falling further from The Divine. I mustn't follow the lies, but cling to the words Elder speaks. The truth. The Divine uses him as a mouthpiece, and I have seen it with my own eyes.

Do not let me doubt you, King.

The impromptu service is well-attended; it appears the entire town has come to listen. I can see from where I stand at the back of the crowd that Elder is pleased, eyes shining as if divinely touched as the folks hang on every word lilting from his lips. My limbs grow restless the longer he speaks, the need to move burning through my muscles.

"Steady," the brethren to my left says in a low undertone. "The time is nigh."

"And now, a chance to redeem your lost souls from eternal damnation," Elder calls, something rapturous rippling through the air among us. A soft humming rises from those around me, and I force myself to join in, slightly off-key from the others.

"Hell waits beyond the veil of this world, and the wolves lurk at the door, lunging for the break in your spiritual defenses. They are patient and endless." Elder's voice cuts through the crowd, and that familiar uncertainty swamps me.

But no.

This is the way.

I had to learn, and so do these sinners.

"You've been chosen by The Divine to fulfill a purpose." Elder lifts bony arms over his head, and we all move as one, enclosing the town in a tight circle. The townspeople murmur, unease spreading like a sickness. Confusion shines in their eyes. Elder was right—here's the proof, right before me. Every one of them should rejoice to have been chosen, for The Divine's plan including them when He didn't have to. Instead, they turn to fear, curling in on themselves as if to ward off an attack. Beginning to protest. A few stand, moving towards my brethren as if to push past. They are surrounded, and The Divine's call cannot be escaped.

It is too late. We are ravenous, but we are not weak. We have been touched by The Divine Himself.

Elder's arms are still over his head. "There will be weeping and gnashing of teeth," he cries out, voice echoing over the now-unrestrained screams of the townspeople. They panic, and my brethren move even closer, laying hands on some, restraining others. Tightening the noose. Slowly the group is forced into two sections—those for service and those for sacrifice.

I take part, nudging a man with gray hair into the group for sacrifice. I do not shirk my responsibility. This is my calling. I've made my choice. And now it is their turn.

"Choose this day whom you will serve—The Divine, or the evil one." Elder's eyes tighten at the corners, sharpening into a fierce look that pierces me to the bone.

I serve The Divine. I will do my duty, King.

The screams of the new recruits echo in my ears, but I focus on Elder. He glows in the darkening sky, fierce in their fervor. "You must choose—life or death?"

It has quieted down as the night progresses. There is still weeping, new brethren sitting in a stupor as their hair comes free in clumps, as the oxen is relieved of its burden of thick robes. I recall how I felt when they came to my town, when they shaved my head. When I ate human flesh for the first time, as The Divine instructed Elder. It is the way.

We lost many of our contemplatives with the famine, but The Divine provided, just as Elder professed He would. Shorn locks scatter the ground, and for a moment I recall the feeling of my own hair, long and shining red in the sun, the texture of it against my fingers.

That girl is no more. Sweat prickles along my scalp, now having been shorn several times on this grand quest. I run my tongue along my teeth, anticipating the amount of provisions we will have for the coming days. Enough to last us a while, I would imagine.

The cookfires roar, great infernos to dispose of the dead—but only after they've been picked clean. Only when they are bones and ragged fragments of whatever clothing we cannot salvage. We need as much food as we can find, especially now that our numbers are swelling once more. The famine forced us to change our ways, and we followed The Divine's command.

Eat and be well.

The soft cries and the scent of cooking flesh beneath gnawing teeth—ripping them from the bones, consuming the unwilling—echo in my ears, fill my nose.

I shove aside the doubt, ignoring the sliver of questions half-formed in my mind, and focus on chewing. Swallowing.

This is the new order. We will eat and be given new life tonight.

All praise to you, King.

A Tale of Two Monks

C.J. Subko

T WO MONKS SAT IN a captured hovel in the village of Strzyboga, drinking ale.

"More ale, Brother Basil?"

"Why thank you, Brother Benedict."

"These Poles are quite troublesome, are they not, Brother Basil?"

"Why yes, Brother Benedict. Indeed, most troublesome. But they will find God in the end."

"Indeed, Brother Basil. They will see the error of their ways."

"And what if any of them were to challenge us, Brother Benedict?"

"Why, I suppose the knights will sort them out soon enough. But I do not think it possible. These lowly, untutored peasants? Who would stand against us?"

Brothers Basil and Benedict had a laugh over their ale, and poured another round.

The tailor Mieszko, a lowly, untutored peasant, stood before a crowded hovel of villagers, hushing them to a tolerable volume.

This was it. This was his moment.

He shook a little as he said, "We must stand against these invaders." It was time. They had taken over their hovels, raided their stores, stolen their property for the Church. It was time to stand. Time to fight.

A ruckus boiled up from the crowd and Mieszko was forced to hush them all again with quivering hands. He swore an oath. Could he not be still? Could they not be quiet? "You're going to wake them!"

The ruckus evaporated, and the big-bellied blacksmith Borosław heaved himself to his feet. Mieszko could feel his toes go numb. Oh, *now* he'd have it. Borosław's voice boomed. "With all respect, Mieszko, who are we against these knights? We say nay and they run us through."

Such a big man, and he was the coward? Mieszko was ashamed of his best friend in this moment. "We are nothing, it is true," Mieszko answered, steadying his voice, "but I do not mean for us to be the sole saviors of Strzyboga. We must make a sacrifice!" He clenched his fists against the shaking. He had to seem strong, assertive.

"A sacrifice?" said the widow Supka shrilly.

Gods! Did no one understand? "To our lord Perun. To fight the invaders!"

Borosław laughed heartily, and was not the only one. "Come now, Mieszko, the gods have not walked the earth since the first age of man. They do not care. They will not come."

Itchy annoyance crimped Mieszko's limbs. He'd expected this pushback, but it didn't make him feel any less foolish. He had not fought when the invaders came, thinking them transient, but his sister had. She had been killed for resisting. And now Mieszko was all that was left. It was his time to say, stand and fight.

Mustering all his courage, he said, "I will make them care! I will make them come." The tittering and side conversations dithered to a halt; everyone was staring at him now, eyes wide.

"Be careful," said the widow Supka. "No one makes the gods do anything. Their whims are not ours to tempt."

Frustrated, Mieszko stumbled into his bachelor's hovel. Gods above, that had gone about as poorly as it could have! He blew the dust off of his little windowsill altar with its stone figurines of Perun and Veles, Marzanna and Mokosh, figures that had been passed down to him from his father and his father and on and on until the generations were too distant to count, like the pinpricks of the stars that now glared down at him menacingly. He gently fingered the divots in their faces and their protruding noses. Would they hear him? Would they heed the words of a quiet little tailor who had never bothered anyone nor asked for anything? Who had never done anything glorious or valorous to deserve their exalted attentions?

He had to try. For his lost sister. For his parents, dead these many years, who would have wept to see their village so ill-used. For himself, who had not stood against the invaders at first, who had welcomed them as friends because he didn't know any better.

With the widow Supka's words repeating in his mind, he burnt a cone of compressed pine resin on a little stone bowl, drinking in its heavy scent. There, that was nice. Calming. Steadying. Holding his palms out at his sides like he had seen the priests do in the temple, he spoke to the empty air, "I ask the Bielobog and Czernobog, I ask Perun and Veles, hear me now in my hour of greatest need. A plague of foreigners has come to Strzyboga. They bring strange words and they encourage us to forsake you. So many have already taken up their cause, but with your help, we could drive them out. We could reclaim the old ways. Please, my lords. Please, Marzanna, Mokosh, Lada, Svarbog. Please do not forsake us."

Letting the pine tar coil up into the realm of Prawia, then he curled up in his bed, alone, as always.

Well, shit. He didn't feel exalted or divine. He didn't feel listened to. He just felt the chill of his bed, and the emptiness of the night.

The first day of Spring came with a bluster and a shock of sunlight cracking through weeks of pregnant dark clouds. Mieszko and Borosław found each other on the way to the river.

"So, have your gods answered?" Borosław teased. Even before the conversions, he had been skeptical of the old ways. Nor did he don the mantle of a Christian. He was a cynic, and it was a wonder to all that he was the best friend of Mieszko the dreamer.

Now his usual levity grated on Mieszko and threw him into a foul temper. How could Borosław be so dense? "You know they haven't. Do you see Lord Perun riding? Do you see Lady Marzanna frost the fields with the breath of winter?"

Borosław laughed a big belly laugh, although his mirth seemed sour. But everything he did was large. "No need to be so poetic, my man. I'm only in jest."

"You're too often in jest."

"And you, not enough."

With a grunt, Mieszko blended in with the crowd amassing at the riverbank, where a giant straw effigy of a woman had been hoisted on a pole. Her hair and apron fanned in the wind. She was Marzanna, goddess of winter, of death. The people of Strzyboga encircled her and raised their fists and spat their prayers—at least, the people who had not taken heart at the wooden cross necklaces offered by the missionaries who promised wealth and eternal life, who drank blood and cannibalized their God and other nonsense.

Mieszko prayed intently; he was angry with the gods, but he would not forsake them yet.

Not yet.

Leopold, karl of the village, stepped forward, wearing a long necklace of braided rushes and wood and bone. He held out his torch. "Today, we count our days differently. Today, we say farewell to the death of winter and welcome the brightness and life of spring, the blessings of our mother Mokosh. Today, we destroy Marzanna!"

A great cry erupted from the crowd. A fervent tear leaked down Mieszko's cheek. Let the gods see, let them see that he kept their rituals, that he deserved their notice!

Like a child watching the ritual for the first time, Mieszko surveyed in wonderment as the karl brought the torch up to Marzanna's skirts. The fabric Mieszko had so carefully sewn himself caught flame, and then the straw that formed her body. The fire crept up inch by inch until the whole of the effigy belched with flames.

Normally, the sight heartened him. The death of winter. The birth of spring. Yet, Mieszko felt a strange surge of discomfort as he watched that fire creep and consume. Everyone else cheered while one of the strong men took hold of the effigy's pole and dunked the whole thing into the river, until it slid off its pole and became suffused, half water half fire, a liminal thing. Yet Mieszko found he could not stop trembling.

"Mieszko," said Borosław. "Mieszko, are you alright?"

Mieszko realized that he had gone quite silent, quite still, while everyone else was cheering.

"They're coming," Mieszko said. "They're coming. They're coming." And he couldn't stop repeating it, couldn't stop staring into that fiery water, until he became aware of a distant thundering behind him. The thunder of footsteps. Of heavy boots running.

"What is happening?" someone shouted.

"They're coming!" Mieszko cried.

And before anybody could run, could think, bulky Teutonic knights in their iron armor and faceless helmets barreled down through the trees and surrounded the mass of worshipers. The man with the longest sword thrust his weapon into the air and announced, "By order of Brother Basil and Brother Benedict and the Teutonic Order, you are to stop this heathen festival and return to your homes! Now!"

Mieszko's breath caught in his throat. All around him, the crowd tautened. A bowstring being pulled. A deer tensing its muscles. Mieszko could feel every breath as it was exhaled from every mouth, the dewdrops still catching in the last of winter chill. Behind him, Marzanna's effigy crackled with the last gasps of fire as it crumpled into the river.

Then, someone snapped the bowstring.

It was simple. It was a rock, pinging against the helmet of a knight. It was a solitary cry.

Mieszko didn't see how it happened but one moment was stillness and another was the thrust of a sword through the belly of a man, a thrust and a twist, and slimy, scarlet entrails spilled onto the ground, the man's desecrated body clanged to its knees, then crumpled to the side. Blood splattered from the withdrawn sword.

A shriek. Another. Then all was chaos, and clanging, and fists banging against temples and blood spraying from mouths, and Mieszko felt himself being pulled away and all he could see was the drowning figure of Marzanna swirling beneath the waters until he was hoisted over a broad shoulder and then it was the ground chasing beneath him, and then a fist, and then he could see nothing at all.

Two monks sat drinking ale in a captured hovel, their frowns deepening with their sips.

"These savages grow restless," said Brother Basil. "Just look how they behaved today!"

"Precisely," said Brother Benedict. "The knights merely came to restore order and they attacked most brutally."

"I think six or seven of the Poles died in the fray," said Brother Basil.

"A shame," said Brother Benedict. "Six souls that will never reach Heaven."

"They should have converted," said Brother Basil, shrugging and lifting his flagon to his lips for a long, slow pull. "We have given them ample time."

"They cling to their old ways like a spider clings to its web," said Brother Benedict.

"And what do we do with spiders, Brother Benedict?" said Brother Basil.

Brother Benedict smiled, a terrible withering smile.

"We lost six," said Borosław, his usual levity corralled behind a deep frown. "Agata was among them." They were a smaller group, now clustered in the hovel.

Mieszko didn't speak, just put a hand on his friend's shoulder. Borosław had been sweet on Agata. Would probably have married her in time. Now she was a cold corpse in an unmarked grave, not even afforded the rites of a proper burial with grave goods and a barrow. Not even given a Christian's dubious burial, as she had never converted. Mieszko, Agata, Borosław, they'd been playfellows as children. Now she was gone. Mieszko's breast twisted with the agony of her absence. She would have been standing near Borosław now, smiling beatifically, keeping the peace between the friends but urging them to fight.

"We must call for the gods again," Mieszko said at last. "They *will* help us. I have prayed to them, but perhaps that is not enough. Perhaps my voice alone is not strong enough." He was desperate now. Pleading. Please. Let them understand. Let them see.

To Mieszko's shock, Borosław and the others nodded. "I see. Then it must be done." And Borosław, who had called the plan silly before, clasped Mieszko's forearm. "I go where you go."

The widow Supka held up a hand. "Go with the gods, young men. But remember what you are calling down."

Mieszko and Borosław skirted the edge of the village. The monks would be drunk at this hour on pilfered honey wine, and the Teutonic knights whoring and making merry. In the minds of the knights, they had won. Strzyborg was but a merry part of the Holy Roman Empire. Why must they patrol in force?

Well. Let them underestimate them, *him.*

Mieszko and Borosław were tiptoeing to the edge of the forest with a hobbled lamb when one of the guards, one who wasn't whoring or drowning himself in drink, stopped them.

Shit. Apparently, not underestimating them enough.

"Men!" barked the guard. "Where go you at this hour?"

"Nowhere in particular!" said Mieszko. "Just out for a fine stroll." The tips of his fingers numbed with anxiety.

"A fine stroll at this hou—"

Borosław's meaty fist cracked into the soldier's temple and floored him.

Mieszko pressed two trembling fingers to the soldier's neck. He could just feel the rabbiting pulse. "Well, he's not dead."

Borosław shrugged. "Well, all your pretty talk was getting us nowhere. Now let's get on with it."

The two men shunted the lamb into the forest, Mieszko closing a hand over its muzzle to stifle its traitorous bleats. They made their way deeper down the path, to the burnt-out ruins that had once been the Great Temple. The wooden stave structure had been the first thing the Christians destroyed, after pillaging its shrines for their statues and breaking them to rubble. Seeing it now, Mieszko felt a flutter in his stomach, the beginnings of rage.

Borosław muscled the struggling lamb onto the center of the stone circle and Mieszko took his knife from his belt. He looked to the sky.

"Lord Perun. Lord Veles. And all the gods and goddesses. Hear us now in our hour of need." He was no priest, but he hoped that speaking from his belly, his heart, would make a difference. It must. "Please. They have killed six already! They will put your people to the sword or convert them to their heathen ways, as they have done in other villages. Help Strzyborg avoid this fate!"

He looked to Borosław. "Good enough, I think."

Mieszko nodded and slashed his knife across the lamb's throat. A luxuriant spray of arterial blood doused him from head to toe.

Borosław laughed heartily and Mieszko glared at him. "This is not the time for levity. If the gods don't answer, it'll be our necks next."

Two monks sat drinking mead in a captured hovel beneath the roiling sky.

"I regret that this is necessary, Brother Benedict," said the first, wiping his sticky mouth with the back of his hand.

"I feel the same, Brother Basil," said the second, tracing his finger around the rim of his flagon.

"I don't know what else was to be expected, Brother Benedict."

"Nor I, Brother Basil. These infidels have been allowed to percolate in their villainy for far too long."

"Ah well, Brother Benedict."

"Ah well, Brother Basil."

Two sons of Strzyboga hunched down in the forest brush beneath a darkened sky.

"Fine night for a battle," said Borosław, patting his belly.

"As fine as we could have wished," said Mieszko with much less panache. For though he hoped himself to be the indomitable warrior, his knees knocked together as they waited in the darkness with fifteen other men and a few women. Coward. He was a coward. Or was he? He was here, wasn't he? That must be enough.

So he waited.

Waited to die. Waited to live. Waited for the promise of a morrow without iron chains and wooden crosses.

A spring bird's whistle punctuated the air. Any native of Strzyboga would wonder what the robin was doing, gracing them with his song so early in the season, and in the night.

It was not a bird, after all. It was the karl. And it was time.

Mieszko slipped quietly behind Borosław, mirroring his steps, a knife in the dark.

A knife with a fluttering heart behind its breastbone.

The barracks were easy enough to find. They were but homes, once, before the knights forcibly removed the residents and claimed them. A small grouping of hovels squatted on one side of the village, now loud with the rustling of horses and the foot-to-foot shuffle of the guard.

The children of Strzyboga crouched in the night, just until the sheen of moonlight caught off a butcher's knife—stabbing straight out of the guard's throat. The man did not, could not scream, just burbled. Blood black in the darkness spurted from the hole in the man's neck as the assassin withdrew his blade and bade his brothers and sisters follow.

And they followed, with butcher knives, cleavers, belt knives, and swords, stealthy as foxes into the henhouse they came.

Mieszko crept past the dying man and bid him fair travels to the world beyond.

Even Christians deserved that pittance.

Mieszko was second into the barracks. The sleeping hulk of a man didn't hear him tiptoeing in. Didn't see or feel him until Mieszko's iron blade kissed his throat and bit in deeper. Although Mieszko's bowels turned towards liquid, he pressed on, flinging the blade in a wide arc, spraying blood through the air as piss trickled down his leg. A droplet of blood painted the cheek of another sleeping knight, who woke just in time for Borosław's cleaver to bury itself into his forehead with a resounding thwack.

Fuck. Mieszko breathed heavy. He had done it. He had killed a man. He'd pissed himself, but he'd done it.

There was no going back now.

Now the knights heard; now they saw their brethren fall beneath the blades of the peasantry they had so reviled. In underclothes, trousers half pulled up, they stumbled from their pallets and scrambled for their swords, but the women they'd bedded held them back, baring their necks to the slaughter. One escaped, grabbed his sword, and made a wobbly thrust at Borosław, who punched him in the face and then slashed him across the throat. Mieszko blinked against the arterial spray and thumbed it across his cheeks. Warpaint, from another time. He and Borosław shared a raider's smile, then fled the hovel with four corpses behind.

Borosław pitched into him; Mieszko stopped short, too late to stop the Teutonic dagger buried hilt-deep in his friend's forehead. Blood glugged from Borosław's mouth, sputtered down his clothes. The knight gleefully pulled his blade free and Mieszko pushed Borosław's body aside and stabbed the knight in the eye, but the ringing in his ears muffled the man's dying shrieks, because Borosław was now crashing to the ground, ungainly and bloody and dead.

No. No! It couldn't be. Mieszko knelt at his side. "Friend! Borosław! Friend!" But there would be no dying words to cling to, for his friend was already gone to Nawia below.

Mieszko bellowed his friend's name, looking up only just in time to see another knight charging him. He hunkered down and the knight slashed his back, splitting his shirt and the skin beneath. Pain lanced across his body, splintered him into shards. He needed to get up. Needed to gain the high ground before he became as cold as Borosław.

A heavy weight thudded atop him. The body of the knight. Mieszko shrugged it off and accepted the hand of Stanisław, the butcher, who yanked him to his feet.

"There are too many," cried Stanisław, whose face sheeted blood from a forehead slice. "Run!"

Mieszko scanned the scene. Everywhere, glints of moonlight revealed Teutonic swords burrowing into his kin's bellies and throats. Knights lay dead on the ground, but not enough, not enough when they were bigger, stronger, more numerous, had extinguished the element of surprise.

Move. Run. Mieszko couldn't *move,* couldn't *run.* His legs were lead, his feet rooted to the ground. What had they done? Shattered a fragile peace into open war and now here lay the consequences, bodies of the children of Strzyboga heaping up in the bloody mud. His bowels were full liquid now, his chest tight and coiled.

Mieszko had done this. Mieszko had been the architect of this doom. He watched and it seemed he could see everything at once, know everything at once. He—

--watched a knight clench his fist around a man's throat and slit the man open cock to chin so his entrails snaked out and glistened red and liquid in the moonlight.

--watched another knight paint a grin across the throat of a shrieking woman, then toss her body aside like a child's ragdoll.

--watched a third knight mash his fist into a man's face again and again until the bones of the man's nose splintered into his pinkish gray brains and blood spewed from his nostrils.

Mieszko wiped blood across his mouth and cried to the sky, "Bielobog and Czernobog, free us from this madness! Gods of Pawia and Nawia, hear my cry!" Then he hurled himself onto the back of a knight, stabbing into the man's brainstem and stabbing again, again, until something solid cracked the side of his head.

The world

dissolved

into the head of a tailor's pin.

The world exploded and expanded.

Mieszko vomited as a knight forced him to his knees. His hands had been bound behind his back, tightly, with thick, scratchy rope.

Mieszko peered out, squinting. Many other men knelt around him, awash in the hesitating light of a burning tree. He could not count. His eyes swam with stars.

Borosław was dead. Stanisław knelt bound beside him.

Mieszko's knees chafed against the gravely earth.

Knights swarmed around to the houses of the village, banging doors, muscling people from their beds until they had amassed a crowd of the whole village before the fated men. Mieszko caught the eyes of Leopold. Shook his head. No. No, don't try to save him. It was too late.

He hung his head. He had failed. He was going to die.

They were all going to die.

And in Nawia, they would know him to be a failure at the last, pissed and shat himself in the heat of battle and shrank away from the final charge.

Two monks stood at the head of a crowd of heathens and Christians. It was difficult to separate which were which, a flock of towheaded, dirty Poles all, except by the crude wooden crosses some of the Christians had fashioned for themselves to wear about their necks.

"What should we do with them, Brother Benedict?" asked Brother Basil.

"Why, I believe we should kill them, Brother Basil," said Brother Benedict.

"You're quite right, Brother Benedict. They've shown themselves to be incorrigible pagans."

Brother Basil thumbed the chin of the man in front of him. A scrawny weasel of a man he recalled to be the town's tailor. The man did not flinch. Dead-eyed already. This chafed Brother Basil.

"Where are your gods now, pagan?" he bellowed into the man's face.

But the man did not flinch.

Well.

Perhaps Brother Basil could not make him flinch.

But he would make him scream.

"This one first," he commanded the knights. A burly Teuton stepped forward and prepared to gut the tailor like a spring salmon.

A flash. A shriek.

"What the devil? Stop—"

The monk's head rolled to the ground.

His headless body stood for another few seconds, blood spurting from the stump.

Then the God of Death kicked his boot against the man's spine and knocked him over.

Mieszko gasped. It could be only Veles, with his face half-charred, half flaring embers, and his antlered head with its tangled black braids, and his eyes swirling all the colors of the worlds here and beyond. He wore a warrior's armor but the black color of grave dirt, and he thrust a sword into the sky and keened.

The keening doubled, trebled, split into a multiplicity of shrieks as the ground yawned open and all the horrors of Nawia roared loose.

Mieszko's heart thundered in his chest, stirred to double-time by fear and awe. A południca wraith with her ragged marriage clothes clawed her way out of the dirt with cracked fingernails, her rotted jaw unhinged and demanding. A strzyga with its lithe, hag's gnarled frame swooped into the sky, white hair floating like a Christian saint's halo around its head, long claws sparkling in their quest for blood. The flaming serpent latawiec uncoiled into an conflagration, sparking fire to the stalks of grass in a sphere around it.

And more, more, all the nightmares of Perun's creation ripping free from the underworld, summoned by their master Veles to battle.

For a moment, time stood still, the monsters hovering, the Christian's tensing, the body of the beheaded monk throbbing.

Then, Veles knelt down and swiped his fingers across the mashed meat, painted the sticky liquid across his pitted cheekbones and eyelids.

No one moved to fight, but the knights crossed themselves. Some of them ran. Brother Benedict sprayed his fellow's blood as he fled with them.

Veles snapped his fingers. The ropes around his subjects' wrists uncoiled and fell to the ground.

"Stand and fight!" he bellowed, in a voice of many voices, of Death itself.

Trembling, Mieszko staggered to his feet and hurled himself at one of the blubbering, praying knights, easily wrenching the sword from his hand.

He had one object.

While next to him the południca slashed her claws and clawed ropes of blood from a Tueton's neck, Mieszko lurched away from the battle in the direction of the fleeing monk. For it was he who had brought the onslaught. He who commanded the knights.

He who, although he had not wielded the blade himself, had wrought the death of Borosław.

And so many people in Strzyboga.

Ahead, the monk tripped, thudding heavily to the ground. He struggled to lurch to his feet, but Mieszko was upon him, kicking him to the ground with a strength he did not know he had.

"Please!" gasped the monk, his lips gaping like a fish's maw, his hands clenched in prayer. "Please, spare me!"

"Where is your God now?" Mieszko cried. "Where is your thirst for death and eternity?"

"Please!" Terror clouded the monk's eyes. "I'm not ready to die."

Mieszko placed the tip of his sword to the apple of the monk's throat. "Offer me the world."

"Everything I have."

"Alright." Mieszko closed his eyes. Then, he thrust the sword into the monk's neck, burying it to the hilt and shredding it out so that the monk's throat severed completely and his head lolled off and thudded to the ground, a poisoned apple to be consigned to Veles.

Mieszko knelt down and dipped his fingertips into the monk's blood, then slashed the sticky, hot liquid across his already-painted cheeks.

Anointed in the blood of his enemy, Mieszko grimly forced his way back into the battle. While Veles' monsters howled and slew, Mieszko slashed and cut and gutted, and together they killed until no Teuton stood alive, until the God of Death and his minions vanished as though they'd never been there at all, until all Strzyboga was free.

Many centuries ago, in a land we now call Poland, in a land we now call Christian, two monks lay dead on the ground, their golden crucifix necklaces stamped into the bloody mud, ravens picking at the jelly of their eyes.

But their lips, purpling and withered?

Were smiling.

BLOOD AND PESTILENCE

ASHLEY GRAVES

MOTHER DIED ON THURSDAY.

The illness came for her swiftly, like a thief in the night. Here one moment, gone the next. Like many of the townsfolk, the great pestilence consumed her body and soul.

Merely a fortnight ago we were joyous.

Papa being a blacksmith meant he always came home smelling of smoke, working around blazing fires. Exhaustion never got in the way of our time as a family—most often spent at the dining table for less than hearty meals. Blacksmiths made a reasonable wage, however famine made certain resources scarce. That eve, when Papa walked through the door with sweat beading down his brow, he wore a jovial grin. He picked Mama up and twirled her in the air.

He told us how he received a bountiful commission, the man compensating him for nearly double the wage per item. The amount he earned was nearly a month's pay. We'd never been wealthy, but we sure felt like royalty that night. Papa treated us to a lavish meal that smelled divine. If I close my eyes, I can still taste the roasted boar and parsnips.

The next week Mama fell ill.

She awoke in the morn with a high fever. A terrible ache plagued her head. Nausea struck soon after and I'd left a chamber bucket by her bed.

I brought her broth made from boiled chicken bones and she'd sit up long enough to muster a few sips before collapsing back down on the bed. Every movement sapped her energy. Her wispy brown hair clung to her sweat soaked skin.

The morrow after brought coughing fits. No amount of water seemed to clear her throat. She began refusing meals, and what little she did take in, she'd soon vomit back up.

It was an illness I'd never seen the likes of in my eighteen years of life.

I'd visit her every hour, bringing a cool, damp cloth to lay on her brow in hopes to lower her fever. Though she adamantly declined food and water, I still encouraged her to take sips of broth.

On the fourth day, painful bumps and boils appeared on her body. The red circles had a shiny purple center. They were everywhere. I found them on her underarms, legs, and neck. I did my best to keep them clean with water and a rag. The infection oozed a sickly green, mixing with crimson blood. It smelled putrid, like fish left out in the sun all day. Mamma looked like a specter with her pale, clammy skin. Dark purple half moons hung under her eyes.

Her coughs stained the rags red. Each rasp stole energy she did not have to spare.

Papa had stopped working. He revealed to me that numerous people in town had fallen ill by the same mysterious disease Mama had contracted. Many had even perished. Worry began to weigh like a millstone in my gut. If the townsfolk were dying, would that mean Mama would die too?

I couldn't envision life without Mama. She was a hard worker and a constant fount of encouragement. She always knew what to say to lift up my spirits. My earliest memory of her was when I was four or five. I'd fallen and scraped up my knee in the yard. Through wails and tears Mama held me, rocking me back and forth while singing softly.

Once she'd finished singing, she kissed my forehead and said to me, "Life is full of hurt, little one, it's how you face it that makes the difference."

For Mama, I tried to face the unknown of this sickness with strength.

Doctors were going around in strange clothing. I'd seen a few pass by the windows in haste.

On the fifth day, a knock came from the door. But I nearly gasped when Papa opened the door and there stood a figure cloaked in black. Atop the doctor's head sat a rounded, black hat. His hands were covered by leather gloves. He carried a cane, and around his neck sat a cylindrical piece of jewelry. Bunches of garlic hung from a rope that dangled from his belt. The most startling piece of his attire, however, was the beak mask over his face. The point was curved and quite long, and the glass eyes were a piercing red.

I know that the doctor should have acted as a glimmer of hope among the dark tide this sickness had brought upon our family, but I couldn't help but feel a twist in my gut as I gazed upon him. His attire reminded me of a raven, a representation of a dark omen descending on the house.

"Have you infected in your residence?" The doctor inquired. He tilted his head and peered past Papa.

"My wife, Alice. She fell ill several days ago and I fear she is on death's door," Papa said, choking back a sob.

"May I examine her?" The doctor asked through a muffled voice.

"Yes, of course. Come in." Father opened the door wider and ushered the man inside. "Please cure her of this wicked ailment."

"Have you or your daughter felt ill?" The doctor asked as we walked to Mama's bedroom.

"No, praise be the Lord. Agnes and I have remained untouched by this wretched illness."

The doctor nodded in acknowledgement of my father's words but did not say anything further. He walked around the house, keeping his distance from us. Every time Papa drew near, the masked doctor took a few steps back. It's as if he already knew we were doomed to follow down Mama's path.

Papa and I watched him as he conducted his physical. With his cane he pulled back the covers. Though Mama was unconscious, I swear I saw her shiver. He used the rod to lift up her shirt and reveal her infected boils. The cane grazed one of the lesions and caused it to rupture. Mama let out a cry and thrashed around for a few seconds.

"Please be careful!" Papa demanded, venom in his voice.

"When did these appear?" He asked with little emotion. As if he'd done this hundreds of times and Mama was not worthy of his time.

Papa clenched his jaw.

"Yesterday. The fourth day of her illness."

The doctor responded with a mere "hmm" and carried out his exam. The cane sunk into the sallow flesh of her stomach; the skin slowly rose to fill the indent he made. She let out a moan and I had to bite my tongue to keep myself from shouting at him to stop.

"She's dehydrated. See how her skin rises slowly? And how prominent the bones are in her face? Is she still eating or drinking?"

"No," I responded. "She's been unable to keep anything down."

After he finished poking and prodding her like cattle, he took us out of the room and shut the bedroom door.

"I believe your wife requires a venesection," the doctor said. His fingers danced on the handle of his cane. The very same cane he just used to prod my mother. I couldn't take my eyes away from it.

"What's that?" I asked, repeating the word in my head.

"It's a procedure in which I make an incision in the vein and allow her to bleed for a measured time. I do this in hopes to rid her blood of the disease. With the tainted blood gone, her body would hopefully make new, healthy blood."

"But won't there still be bad blood in her? Surely you cannot drain all her blood and expect her to live?" I asked. I could hear the worry in my voice.

"I plan to drain just enough blood where the good will outweigh the bad," he replied with confidence.

Papa reluctantly agreed. He just wanted Mama better.

The doctor entered her room on his lonesome, insisting that he needed complete focus to perform the procedure. Papa and I sat on the settle while we waited. He held me in a hug while tears rolled down my cheeks and dripped off my chin. Every moan or gasp we heard led him to hold me tighter.

"We will get through this, Agnes. The Lord will abide," he whispered as he kissed my forehead.

"He will abide," I agreed emptily. Right now He couldn't feel farther away.

When finished, he emerged from the room smelling of rust and garlic.

"She's resting now. I can only hope I was not too late."

"Thank you, Doctor," Papa said.

"I wouldn't thank me so soon. She will need to be confined to this household for forty days. You two must remain in confinement as well. I would strongly suggest covering your faces when caring for her. She is highly contagious. You may already be infected." His beak lowered for a mere moment.

"Yes, sir." Papa nodded. "If one of us falls ill, how should we send for you?"

"I'll do my best to return in a few days. Until then, rinse your hands constantly and don't forget the mouth coverings."

Mama died the next day.

We found her in the morning, blood staining the pillows and sheets. Papa wrapped her in a layer of linen while sobbing uncontrollably. I begged for tears to come, and they did eventually, but at first I felt nothing. I was empty inside. Like something had reached way down inside me and ripped out the pieces that made me who I am.

I just sat in front of the hearth for hours, staring into the open flames. I wondered if I stuck my hand in the flames if it would help me feel again.

Before we could arrange a funeral Papa fell ill. The same ailments that afflicted Mama ravaged him. I prayed that getting him treated more urgently than Mama would help. I waited by the window in hopes to see a doctor pass by. The cobblestone streets stayed empty.

How could one illness change our way of life so quickly?

On the second day of Papa's illness I saw the familiar cloak and beak. I nearly hesitated. The last doctor did not live up to his promises of healing. How could I be sure this one would be any different.

Papa's cough steeled my resolve. I was unsure if it was the same doctor who previously visited us, but I didn't care. Right now I needed help.

I flew from the window, the curtain swaying in the breeze I conjured. Throwing open the door, I shouted for the doctor to come post haste. I could tell I gave the poor doctor a fright. He insisted I return to my home. His muffled voice sounded similar, yet he said this was his first time passing through this part of the city.

"Please, come quick," I entreated him. "My Mama perished and now my Papa has taken ill."

The man cocked his head to the side, listening adeptly to my tale. Finally he nodded and followed me in.

My nose must have adapted to my brief exposure to fresh air because when I stepped back into my dwelling I nearly gagged. A scent so foul permeated my nostrils. It was putrid, as if I'd forgotten to change the chamber bucket for many days. As if a meal had gone sour and sat for weeks. Mama had begun to smell.

A tapping on my shoulder made me turn around. The doctor had poked me with his cane to capture my attention. I shuddered, thinking of how the cane had nearly pierced Mama's skin. How many others had he touched with that cane?

He reached to his waist and broke off a piece of garlic.

"Crush it and smear the garlic under your nose. It'll help block out the stench," he instructed.

While the overpowering smell was not much better, I did as he instructed. It burned and brought tears to my eyes. Although, with everything that had happened, the tears may have already been there.

"Where is your mother?" He asked.

"Papa and I wrapped her in cloth and moved her to my room."

Since then I've been sleeping on animal skins in front of the fire. The cold, uncomfortable floor had left an ache in my back.

"And your father?"

"Where Mama had been. We had no other place where he could rest and we figured he already had what Mama had."

"I see."

The crackling fire filled the silence as we stared at one another. He looked so familiar, though it must just be the attire. I wondered how many doctors there were roaming around the city. His gaze fell on the animal skins on the floor.

He surveyed the room, taking it all in. From the flames to the iron cauldron hanging in the kitchen.

He cleared his throat. "Once I finish examining him and leave here I will send for people to collect your mother. Unfortunately, I cannot say your mother will be buried in an individual plot. With so many dead, I fear there are not enough gravediggers healthy enough to complete the task. Instead, they've been ordered to place the dead in a mass grave."

Something warm hit my cheek and I realized I was crying once again. Mama would not have a proper burial. I would not have somewhere to go and honor her. And if Papa did not get better, I would be alone.

If I too did not fall prey to this disease sent about by Satan himself.

Like Mama, the doctor examined Papa with a cane. He hovered over Papa like a death angel.

"When was the last time he ate?" The doctor lifted Papa's blankets off him and pulled back his shirt with the rod.

"Yesterday," I said standing at the foot of the bed. " He refused food this morning and began coughing."

"Can you tell me the symptoms of your mother before her passing? I did not see her prior."

I quickly explained everything that had ailed her.

"I see. With your permission I would like to conduct the venesection on him. His symptoms, it sounds, are not as far progressed as your mother's. He may fare a better chance."

I swallowed. It was hard not to correlate Mama's demise with the arrival of the doctor and his methods. However, Papa seemed to quickly be following in her footsteps. Without medical help I may lose him as well. "How can I know this will succeed? With Mama it only seemed to weaken her. She was gone the next day."

He lowered his cane and replaced Papa's blankets. "I can see why you may have hesitation. But in my opinion it sounds like your mother's condition was too far progressed for the treatment to work. I believe that your father may stand a better chance since he is still in the early stages of the illness."

I let out a deep breath. "With your permission, may I be allowed to observe the treatment?"

He shook his head. "This procedure requires focus and can easily be contaminated. I will have to ask you to wait out here."

A deep rattle came from Papa as he broke out in a coughing fit.

"Okay." I gazed at Papa. The sickness was overtaking him fast. "I give you my permission."

It felt like I waited for ages for the doctor to exit the bedchamber. For a while, I watched the flames dance across the logs in the fireplace. The crackling helped quell the rapid beat of my heart.

Without the distraction of caring for Papa, I felt the weight of the past week's events pressing on me. Mama was gone. Her body in my room. She won't get a proper burial. Instead she'll be thrown in a pit with others.

Just another death to add to the toll.

And what if Papa doesn't recover? What if his sickness worsens? I'll be left alone. I'd never been spoken for. No husband waiting for me.

Who am I without them?

My stomach turned and I felt light headed. The stew I had for lunch came up in a rush. I barely made it to the waste bucket in the kitchen. Grabbing a cloth, I wiped the thick residue from my chin.

A thud from the bedroom made me startle. I clutched my chest, my heart thundering loudly. What was that? Maybe the doctor had just dropped something upon finishing Papa?

I stood, smoothing my skirts. A glance out the window revealed that night had fallen. I should've lit some candles instead of wool gathering in front of the fireplace.

My curiosity got the better of me. Carefully, I stepped on the floorboards, knowing which ones creaked. Pressing my ear against the cold wood, I listened for any further sounds.

A sucking noise came from within the chamber.

Taking a deep breath, I gently pushed the door open. An icy chill slithered down my spine as I took in the sight before me. All the blood in my body rushed to my feet, leaving gooseflesh in its wake. The plague doctor's beak sat on the floor by the bed. I'd guess that was the noise I'd heard earlier since the mask still rocked back and forth ever-so-slightly.

A pale, ashen figure crouched over Papa. Rows of sharp teeth dug into the flesh of his arm as the creature fed upon his blood. The figure's ears were pointed, rather noticeable with the lack of hair on its head.

"Stop it! Leave him be!" I shouted before I could stop myself. I'm unsure where my boldness came from because I wanted nothing more than to flee in terror.

The man–or creature–stood quickly, turning to face me with my papa's blood coating its mouth and chin. A forked tongue slipped past its lips and lapped up the residue.

A snake-like hissed passed from its lips.

I grabbed the candle holder off the table near the door and swung at the beast.

"Be gone, foul demon. I revoke your welcome in this house." I brandished the candle holder again, hitting the beast in the head. Black rivelets of blood dripped from the wound.

It hissed at me again. "You'll regret that."

Before I could swing again the creature rammed into me, knocking me to the ground. My back hit the floor hard and all the air in my lungs vacated my body in a surprised gasp. It ran past me and out the front door before I could even stand up.

I tried hard to catch my breath, taking in quick gasps. The air I sucked in was cold and tasted coppery.

I surveyed the room, hoping to find something to focus on to ward off the black specks encroaching my vision. The bird mask lay on the floor still, the creature having forgotten it in its haste.

Once my breathing slowed, I stood and stumbled over to Papa. He was still breathing but it was much shallower now. Taking the damp rag out of the water bowl on the nightstand, I covered the wound on his arm and held pressure.

"Alice? Alice is that you?" Papa asked, his eyes still closed. Beads of sweat rolled down his pallid brow.

"No, Papa. It's me, Agnes. Please hold still so I can help you."

He began fidgeting, trying to pull away from my touch. His skin beneath my fingers was ice cold. My heart sank. How could someone–something do this?

I swaddled Papa in blankets in hopes to warm him.

"Alice, make it stop! It burns. My arm's on fire." His eyes opened wide and made contact with mine. There was no recognition in his gaze, only terror.

He thrashed around for another minute before breaking out into a coughing fit that sapped the rest of his energy. With him at rest, I left the room in search of wound dressing. I found clean linen in the wash room along with some aloe. I returned and cleaned the wound. Several puncture marks oozed blood. Black lines stemmed from the wound. Their shape reminded me of barren tree branches.

I wrapped my father's arm with the bandage material I gathered. He still lay there, in a sleep that mirrored death. Occasionally his head would move side to side and he'd mumble incoherently in his sleep. His skin was still cool to the touch. I placed some warm rags on his forehead in hopes to raise his temperature. It was up to me now to try and help him. I wouldn't be able to trust any more doctors.

What was that thing? I'd never heard or seen anything like it in my life.

I closed my eyes and massaged my temple with trembling hands. What was I to do? So much had been thrust upon me all at once. It nearly felt like too much for one person to bear.

My breath began quickening. Pressure built in my lungs and my heart beat so rapidly I thought it would explode. Black vines crept into the edge of my vision, threatening to overtake it completely. The room around me faded from view. All I knew was the thunderous beat of my heart.

Mama used to call these my worry spells.

"Agnes," she would say, putting her hands on my shoulders, "you're worrying again. Close your eyes."

I did, shutting out my father's blurry image.

"Count to three and then think of something that makes you smile."

I mumbled the numbers under my breath and pictured the time I had a herd of goats following me around my Uncle's farm. I was small, maybe six, carrying hay and the goats all gathered around me bleating. They tried to steal the straw from my hands, their lips and breath tickling my fingers. I think that was the hardest I'd ever laughed in my life.

"Now I'm going to count to three again and you can open your eyes. One, two, three..."

The last word is whispered in my ear. I feel the breath on my ear as I rip my eyes open. There's nothing in the room. No one behind me.

I poked my head out the bedchamber's door. In all the confusion I'd forgotten that the entry way had been left wide open when the creature departed in haste. The inky darkness of night loomed just outside, and my home was open to whatever lurked in the streets.

I stepped toward the doorway, feeling the coolness that nightfall had brought. Gooseflesh prickled my skin.

The streets were silent. No hooves trotting on the pavement from late night travelers. No idle chatter from passerbys.

I closed the door and turned the lock. I'd be inviting no one in without seeing their true face first.

I figured sleep would be hard to come by with the memory of that creature still fresh on my mind, but I believe the exhaustion of caring for my parents had caught up with me. One minute I was staring into the flames and the next I was being awoken by a repetitive sound.

It was a hollow sound, coming in threes.

Could it be Papa knocking on something to get my attention? I walked to the bedchamber, but stopped once I heard the sound again. It was coming from behind me.

I scanned the room. Once my gaze landed on the window my blood ran cold. Standing just outside the glass was the creature from earlier. It still stood adorned in its robe. A sinister, pointed grin spread across its face. In one hand it used the cane to tap on the window. The other hand held something I couldn't quite make out at first. Then my eyes adjusted to the dim light and I stumbled backward, tripping and falling hard on the ground.

Its right hand held another beaked mask. Only this mask still had a severed head attached to it. Blood still dripped from the torn skin of the neck.

Once the creature knew it had my full attention, it ripped the mask from the head and tossed the flesh aside. It took the beaked mask and slid it back over its own head. Then it gave me a wave and walked away from the window.

I didn't know I was breathing so hard until I began clawing at my throat for air.

Sleep evaded me the rest of the night. Every time I closed my eyes the image of the severed head stared back at me. Instead I kept vigil over my Papa, tending to him. I knew that if I tried to talk to someone about what transpired last night, regarding both my father and the incident at the window, that they would think me mad. They'd believe I'd caught the illness and had gone delirious with fever.

And sure enough, fever struck me the next morn as I forced broth into my Papa's mouth. His breath had become shallower. It started out as weakness. I figured I'd just over exerted myself with the terrible events of the previous night. Then the ache settled into my bones. My skin turned warm and all my strength fled from my body, just as the creature had fled from Papa's room.

Something deep down in my gut told me this is what the creature wanted. What it was waiting for. Why fight your prey when you can just take advantage of them when they are weak and at your mercy? How many of the deaths were actually from the illness itself? What if many of them were from this beast, going door to door and sucking the life force from these sickly people? Could one creature be responsible for so many deaths? Or were there more using the same disguise?

I pushed through the weakness and tended to my Papa a few more times that day. I made sure we both ate the stew I'd made the day prior.

By the time night fell, I found myself trying hard to stay awake. I knew the creature was lurking somewhere, waiting for me to fall asleep. The tickle in my throat kept me coughing, which helped for a little while. Eventually, my body did succumb to slumber.

I awoke to a sharp, burning pain on my neck. Pressure pinned my body down. My eyes flew open and I didn't wait, I took the fragmented chicken bone I'd armed myself with earlier and plunged it into whatever was on top of me.

A loud hiss erupted from the creature as it clutched its ribs and stumbled backward toward the fire. The creature caught itself before falling into the flames. Its gaze fell upon me. Its red irises burned into my soul. Behind them I saw destruction. I saw cities littered with dead and buildings engulfed in flames.Rats feasted on rotten corpses laid out in the streets, their eyes red like the creatures. Flies buzzed in my ears. I saw them land on the dead and lay their eggs in their eyes, ears, and mouths. Maggots emerged and devoured flesh.

"You see what I can do, child? I bring plague and destruction to cities and feast upon all who are weak. Both your father and mother tasted marvelous. Your blood however," he stepped closer, licking his lips, "is divine. I will take great pleasure in draining you dry."

He ripped the fragmented bone out of the side of his ribcage and threw it to the ground.

"Leave us alone!" I screamed. Blood trickled from the side of my neck, staining my white chemise. My scream brought back the tickle in my throat and I broke out into a coughing fit.

It took advantage of my weakness and struck. Sharp talons had taken the place of gloved hands. The claws raked my abdomen and I felt as if I'd nearly been split in two. Fire blazed across my stomach. My knees buckled and I collapsed to the ground.

Waves of heat rolled over me from the fire burning bright in the hearth. The sweat on my brow from fever now doubled. During the struggle, one of us must have knocked over the stand containing firesticks. Several wooden sticks lay strewn about the floor.

I reached for one just as I was ripped backward. The creature was upon me again.

"Keep struggling," it mused. "It only makes your blood richer. I think that's one of the things I miss the most about the hunt. I miss the thrill. The chase."

I felt its tongue lap the sticky blood from my neck. I used this as a distraction to reach for the fire sticks.

It sighed. "If only I could preserve you."

The tip of my finger brushed against a sharp wooden tip.

"Alas, you'd fade too fast."

The creature clamped its jaws back on the tender wound of my neck just as I grasped my weapon. I gasped loudly, turning my inhalation into a battle cry as I drove the stick into the creature.

The sharp teeth unclamped from my neck and the being went stiff. Its weight fell upon me, crushing me. A sweet copper taste mixed with the salty taste of sweat in my mouth. My stomach turned as the creature's blood slipped down my throat, yet sickness did not come.

Shoving the beast off me, I laid there, sucking in rapid breaths. Another worry spell at the worst moment. I closed my eyes and once again pictured happier memories–this time it was of Mama and Papa. That last feast before the sickness struck.

My breathing began to slow. I tried to open my eyes, but they had grown heavy. Darkness had taken me over.

Morning light woke me. The bright beams peered through the curtain and nearly felt as if they were burning my skin. My body felt as if it weighed a thousand pounds.The blood flowing through my veins burned. I was hungry. Famished.

I sat up. The smell of iron filled my nostrils and for some reason my hunger flared. Peering to my right, I saw the withered body of the beast that had plagued my family. The fire stick I'd defended myself with had lodged itself into one ear and emerged out of the other.

The events of the night came back to me. I touched my neck to feel the wound the monster had left behind. Only...there was nothing except the crusted flakes of dried blood. I did the same with my abdomen, again the wound had healed. How was this possible?

I ran to the kitchen and grabbed the nearest metal pot. I screamed and dropped it when I saw the reflection. My skin was ashen. My teeth sharp.

I had become like the creature.

A noise startles me from the bedchamber. Papa. In everything I'd forgotten about him.

I rushed to the room, recoiling at the bright sunlight filling the area. Carefully, I shut the curtains and turned to look at Papa. Pustules covered his face, arms and legs. The arm that the creature had drank from earlier had black lines running up his veins. He moaned in pain.

"Oh Papa," I cried. How quickly he had fallen to the plague.

I stepped closer but stopped. The smell of iron hit me once more. It caused my teeth to ache and my belly to burn. Blood oozed from a boil on the side of Papa's face.

I looked away. Saliva filled my mouth.

I needed to leave.

I ran–faster than I'd ever ran–toward the door. But when I threw the door open it felt like I'd jumped into a blacksmith's fire. The sun was too bright.

I backed away, smoke rising from my skin. Once I'd reached a dim area I felt normal again. The smoke stopped spiraling upward from my ashen flesh.

How had the creatures moved around in daylight earlier? I thought for a moment before the answer struck me.

The beaked outfit.

The garments had covered the creature head to toe, protecting it from the sunlight.

"Alice?"

My Papa's voice was merely a whisper.

I ventured back into Papa's room to find his eyes opened a sliver. I wondered if he thought I was a delusion brought about by fever.

"End it. Please."

I swallowed hard.

"Papa, no." My raspy voice was not my own. I sounded like I hadn't drank in days. " I can help you." Even I knew it was a lie the second it left my lips.

"End it," he said again as a plea. He broke out into a coughing fit and blood sprayed from his mouth, staining the sheets red.

The smell was overwhelming. A force against my own will pulled me forward.

"Please," he begged.

My hand—now equipped with its own sharp talons—caressed his face. He coughed again, sending blood droplets onto my cheek. Something primal in me took control. My sharp teeth tore into his neck. The sweet taste of metallic blood filled my mouth. I couldn't get enough. I drank and drank until the well ran dry.

WITH THE TONGUE

JULIA JACKSON

THE CARVINGS DRINK MY blood. Drops of red absorbed by the white stone I've given everything to. *Everything.* Even the blood spattered before me. I study my shaking hands as I crouch on the ground, a display of overlapping scars and fresh pink cuts upon the flesh of a failed artist.

This is the first time the work didn't come easy. It won't come to me at all. My talent has far surpassed anything expected of a lowly orphan of the church. Until this sculpture, laughing in my face, mocking what I once was.

The entrance to the cathedral should be a vision of beauty. It is here that the devout stand upon the precipice of being closer with the one true God. Where *I* transition from the stench of the rat-infested streets, over the threshold to solace and salvation. It is my duty to surround this door of wood and iron with marble sculptures reflecting the likeness of Saints.

I try. Time and time again I try to carve. To chisel. To break into the stone only to make it smooth again. She just doesn't look right. None of the figures do. They look more like masks, a comedy at the theater, characters playing a charade.

"Giovanni. What—what is this swine?" The Priest appears, spits on the stone next to me. I continue to kneel before my failed attempt, while peering up at the man of cloth, his mouth pulled into a sneer.

His own sigh of disappointment meets the back of my neck, hotter than the scorching sun shining down upon the steps of the cathedral.

"My—"

"I do not wish to hear your excuses." He kicks me square in the back. I am grateful to already be on my knees, though the pain that shoots up to my skull burns no less. "You should be full of shame for making a face more akin to a beast than a Saint."

My chin drops deeper into my chest. A thickness in my throat building from the sheer horror of disappointing the man that practically raised me. Father is right. Our Lord would be disappointed in my young hands being so unsure.

He softens. "Come, Giovanni. Join me at the altar. There is no better place to find your inspiration again." Father Vitale's cold, bony hand finds my shoulder, as if healing the pain he just inflicted.

Father cares for me.

He loves me.

Father's feet shuffle across the stone, and he moves in front of me, into the depths of the Cathedral. There is silence as his silhouette fades into the distance, until his frail voice calls back to me, "God will show you the way if you only open your eyes."

I stand, inverting my back and reaching my arms out. I look up to the sky and stretch out the pose I've held all morning working on the Saint's face.

My finger traces her nose—crooked. Her left eye—squinted. An uncontrolled moan escapes my lips, fingers curling into fists at my sides, ready to punch the stone.

If only I could see her face clearly in my mind. If only God would speak to me.

One of the diseased coughs behind me. Four of them lay on the steps this morning, their bodies wasting to frailty and decomposing in the sun. They usually arrive at the Cathedral when they reach the point of teetering between life and death, never to leave again. One last opportunity to repent for their sins before meeting their maker. Before disease consumes their mortal bones.

They sicken me. The bubbling wounds splayed across their faces and the fumes that rise from their skin stir my stomach. I swallow down the contents threatening to spew from my mouth. My feet can not move quick enough after Father Vitale, who steps over the sick as though they are nothing.

The confines of the Church have been my refuge the entirety of my life. Each step through this space of worship, between the floor to ceiling columns and pews, fills me with warmth. I created this. Or, at least, I made it as beautiful as it is now.

Corners of the Cathedral are pitch black, but the glorious stained-glass windows of green and red stream in the sun's glowing rays, illuminating all that my gifted hands have sculpted. I was the one that engraved the scriptures on the marbled walls. I have broken many fingers chiseling into the stone of grand archways to tell the stories of God, bringing the tree of knowledge of good and evil, the sacrifice upon the cross, and everything in between to life.

The echoes of Father Vitale's conversation with a woman in rags bounces off the walls—off my artwork. Smoke wafts from the altar at the front of the room, the familiar scent of incense singing in my nose—frankincense, cypress, myrrh.

Sweat drips from my temple.

I am an artist. A great artist.

What went wrong, God? I have not changed my methods. I have remained devout to the word of the Bible. Yet, I draw a blank in my mind.

Prayer. *Prayer* is what I need for answers. To see the vision of the Saint as she is meant to be carved. As to not disappoint Father. He continues to speak with the woman, a hand upon her shoulder in comfort while a furrowed brow frames the disdain within his eyes. I try not to listen in, instead folding my hands in prayer and bowing my head.

"God, why have you forsaken me?" On a breath I whisper the words, so that no one but the Lord may hear. "Am I not one of your children, whom you have blessed with not only life, but the skill of an artist? Have I not devoted my innocent hands to be torn and calloused in the name of sharing your stories with the world? Why, God, why have you built such indestructible walls? How is it fair to bestow upon me the vision to see and then create, only to take it away when I need it most? Father will kick me again. Again and again and again. Maybe next time down the stairs to die with the sickening souls that lay splayed upon the Cathedral steps." I shift in the wood pew and wipe the sweat from my palms on my robes before moving them back to prayer. "You must allow me a vision, must allow me to impress Father Vitale. Please, God, *please.* I will do anything."

I pinch my eyes tightly, holding back the tears that want to break free.

"Anything," the promise escapes my raw throat at a high pitch. "*Anything.*"

"You must help my son!" The woman falls to her knees, clinging to Father's robe. He pulls it away from her.

"I do not have the power to do anything. Allowing him within the walls of the Cathedral will not heal your diseased son. He must repent on the steps with the rest of them. He must hope that the divine Saint Mary will be gracious enough to come down and lick his wounds."

Her breath catches in her throat, the poor woman's face colored a faint green. "Lick his wounds?"

"Yes, my child." Father's hand reluctantly rests upon the crown of her head, his face cringing as it makes contact with her greasy mess of silver hair. "It is known by my brethren that Saint Mary will save souls that deserve more time in this world by way of healing with her tongue. Her licking upon an open wound works miracles. It connects the dying soul with God, bringing them back to life."

My stomach lurches as I picture the outline of a beautiful Saint bathed in white light, placing her tongue anywhere near the putrid faces of the diseased—the many illnesses that run rampant upon the village, inescapable and unforgiving.

My bones quiver, but the woman stands, a smile of hope painted across her lips.

Father Vitale catches me watching. I avert my eyes to the altar, focusing on the golden chalice, then the flickering flame that heats the candle wax, spilling it onto the scarlet fabric below. He clears his throat, so I turn all my attention to my bloody hands. I fumble aimlessly through my mind for passages of the Bible to distract me, but the words Father spoke of Saint Mary play in my head.

"Thank you, *thank you*. I will pray to Saint Mary. I have faith my son will be saved," the woman says as they walk past me, Father ushering her out.

"Whatever is God's will, shall be," he says.

God's will.

May God's will speak to me through the passages I have memorized.

I suddenly recall 1 Corinthians 14:2. *For one who speaks in an unknown tongue does not speak to people but to God; for no one understands him or catches his meaning, but by the Spirit he speaks mysteries, secret truths, hidden things.*

Saliva builds in my mouth. I trace the back of my teeth with my tongue, contemplating hidden things. The vision of the Saint I am to sculpt is a mystery to me, shrouded in darkness, eluding me to the point of failure.

Maybe it is Saint Mary herself, too busy licking wounds to show her face to me. Perhaps it is her I am to connect with. Who I need to pray to.

An itch burrows into my mind, scratching deeply, trying to get me to see something.

"Anything, God," I promise again, staring up at the ceiling, then remember another passage within the Great book.

James 3:5 says, *In the same way, the tongue is a small part of the body, but it boasts of great things. Consider how small a spark sets a great forest ablaze.*

Running my hands through my hair, I listen to that itch, now scraping within my skull. There is power in the tongue. *Of course.* Power of speech, but what if there's more? What if there's more within those wounds? What if I may capture the essence of–

No.

It could not be.

I try to see her face again. Saint Mary. Licking at their wounds. I can't see her face. I still can't see her blessed face!

But... if I were to lick the same wounds she had, could I be connected to her? Could I see her face?

No.

Yes.

I bite my knuckle, hand gripped so tight patches of white appear.

Bells ring out, vibrating their chimes like a sign direct from angels. This is Divine intervention. An answer to my prayers.

Pinpricks in the fabric of the dark sky shimmer above. I sit in wait, hidden in the shadow of the Cathedral, watching the poor souls lay dying. A light appears, shining down on a woman with hair as black and slick as the feather of a crow. White brilliance from the moon, or from the Saint herself, falls on her.

Thank you, God. Thank you.

I pull my black cloak high on my head, making sure my face is covered as I creep toward the woman. The moment I sit beside her, I recoil, turning my head to breathe in my own cloak in search of reprieve from the woman's horrible smell. Her rotting flesh, roasted in the sun all day.

With strength, may we receive greatness. With sacrifice, may we receive blessings.

I search our surroundings as I turn back to the woman. Nobody need bear witness to this. It is only her and I, save the other bodies only a few steps away, but I know they are too close to the brink of death to know what is going on around them.

I fiddle with the hem of my hood, unease settling upon me. But then I see her. The sculpture at the door, judging me and my weakness, urging me to sacrifice.

Matted hair on the woman's cheek covers her biggest wound. Brushing it away with my fingertips, I pray. *Saint Mary, may you have already licked this wound. May I be connected to you through this woman's healing.*

The smell of decay intensifies as I draw nearer. The festering wound appears to have a pulse of its own—a heartbeat on her cheek, in rhythm with her slow, dying heart.

Her entire face is covered in bumps. Some small, red, and angry. Others enlarged and full of puss, the yellow fluid pushing its way to the surface, ready to burst.

But this one—the one on her cheek—is the largest of them all, spreading near the entirety of her right cheekbone. The flesh has been split open, blood swelling around a bubbling pink substance. It begins to throb faster, and puss weeps from it, down her face and over the corner of her mouth.

I lick my lips, and lean in.

The wound is warm on my tongue. Warm and wet. Something burns in my throat, but I ignore it and lick more, lapping up the puss and blood. Swallowing the sour fluid that oozes out of the flesh when my tongue adds pressure to it.

Every part of my being wants to spit it all out as I move away from her, walking backward, up the steps. But I don't, for I fear that it will disconnect me from Saint Mary.

I curl into myself beside the door to the Cathedral, beside my carvings. And I pray until sleep takes me.

The hot sun burns my skin. I wake to this, along with a vile taste in my mouth and aching eyes. How long have I been asleep for?

I attempt to stand, but my head spins too fast and I return to the stone beneath me. My body feels lost in a haze, yet I manage to see movement before me. A woman. Sitting on the steps. *The* woman. Someone gives her water, and she sips it gratefully. My jaw falls agape.

She stands. Father's words were true—Saint Mary heals! The woman is healed miraculously, walking up the church steps that were so close to being her final resting place.

She is healed!

Which means—

I could jump for pure joy if my feet were steady enough to allow it. Instead, I crawl to my tools, unfolding the fabric holding the metal chisels in place.

Crystalline light fills my mind and I see the heart-stopping gaze I have been so desperate to view. The Saint's eyes are big and wide, revealing green with threads of gold, and the smallest black dots in the middle. Her lashes are long and protective of such enchanting beauty.

Tears stream from the corners of my own eyes as the smallest chisel appears in my hand. The tool is ready to work, and so am I.

It's all so effortless. Metal meeting stone, tapping repeatedly, scraping the perfect lines of the vision I saw of Saint Mary. Her eyes are perfect. Even. Bright and open to the world. To her miracles.

I blow upon the creation that has appeared by the grace of God. Dust flies into the air, tickling my face and I can't help but laugh. God is good. God did not forget about me afterall. Glory be to God.

"This is better." I jump at the voice, despite its small, hoarse tone.

"Father Vitale." My head bows. "I do hope this pleases you."

"Yes. These eyes," he fingers the hollow space above the eyelid, "these eyes are much better. They reflect a Saint, not swine like they once did."

"Thank you, Father."

"Do not thank me yet, Giovanni. There is much work to be done." With that, he walks away as if the conversation had not happened at all.

Panic slithers through me. I only saw the eyes in my vision. Father is right. I have more to see. I think of James 3:9-10 *With the tongue we bless our Lord and Father, and with it we curse men, who have been made in God's likeness. Out of the same mouth come blessing and cursing.*

I bless my Lord through my words and prayers. And now my tongue is a blessing. God has shared with me a new gift, and with strength of will, I can now see more of the Saint, and one day be the best artist of this world.

Night after night, I feast upon the wounds of the diseased. Suckling at the puss like a newborn pup.

Each morning I awake with stronger visions, despite nobody else recovering apart from that first woman. It does not matter, though, because Saint Mary continues to speak to me. Flashes of her face become more and more clear. So much so that I grow dizzy when I'm not working on the sculpture. The images are so strong they cause me to be ill, but I always manage to empty the contents of my stomach away from my sculpture of her precious face.

Father has been so impressed, watching as layer after layer of dust is removed from the stone, revealing work that is greater than I have ever been able to create.

I barely leave the sculpture. I remain here at the threshold to the Cathedral, carving by day and feasting on flesh at night. One man, barely older than I, struggled against me as I began to run my tongue across his chin. I hit his head upon the steps, my hunger for inspiration controlling my hands.

He would have died anyway. God already decided it was his time.

As blood spilled from his head and my tongue pushed deep within his skin, I wondered if he was the son of that desperate woman who begged with Father that first day Divine inspiration struck.

As I work the next day, my breath is hard to come by. My chisel keeps falling from my hands, and my visions go from bright and clear, to speckled and full of stars—just as I had seen the first night I used my tongue to connect with God.

If only evening would fall, so I could lick more of those dying around me. That would give me strength to continue on.

Barely able to stand, nor breathe, I allow the spinning world to consume me and close my eyes. Just for today, I would allow myself to rest.

"It is a shame." A voice. Far off in the distance. "He has been speaking nonsense for three days, and then his face began to blister."

Something hard hits my chest, rotating my body face up.

"I had taken him in since he was a boy. Saw his potential." Father Vitale. It's Father Vitale's voice. He is close now. A comfort to the thrumming pain in my body. Why am I in so much pain? I have work to do, God.

"It was his hands that sculpted so much of this Cathedral, you know. Its beauty is thanks to him. And now—now the disease has ravaged him. Left him useless and dead on our doorstep like all the other diseased."

A pressure turns me onto my side. A kick, square in my back, sends me toppling down the stairs, the stone cutting me over and over again. Taking more from me. Taking everything.

I hear the unmistakable sound of Father spitting down upon me.

He...

Unable to move my body, or even to blink, my eyes gape up at the sky, burning.

I...

I'm so cold. So cold, and the terror begins to swallow me whole.

"What a waste. Dead before he finished his masterpiece."

Anything.

I had promised anything to God.

Please, God, please. Let the rats take me now, before a tongue may touch my face.

The Beast and the Maid

Teagan Olivia King

I N THE DARKNESS, ON the far side of the red mist, there is a girl with a sword in her hand. And she is singing.

Her notes are like honey, dripping down the charred stone walls, gathering like shadows in the low places. She does not know the words. The song does not have them. Only sound, thick like fresh blood slipping from a wound. A power quickens in her veins–a hunger–the red mist before her tightening and stretching like skin. This is what she was taught by the one who came before her, the Warden who died in a flash of flayed flesh and tearing claws. She remembers his tears, his eyes, how they stared up at her in that final moment and she watched the pain turn to relief as the breath escaped his lips like puffs of candle smoke.

Now, it is just her. The hunger. And the song she seems to know by heart. She raises her voice, fingers tightening around the rusted hilt of the sword. Its blade was how the last Warden traveled through the mist. Slashing the curtain of undulating crimson and stepping through to meet the Beast. But the girl is scared. She knows what the Beast can do. The last Warden's body still lays crumpled in one corner of the room, bones split and cracked like a carcass picked over by crows. She does not know how to use the sword, other than to swing and pray to the Saints the Beast will not hurt her.

But the Saints do not listen. They haven't for a long time and the girl knows she is alone in this. When it comes time to face the Beast, the Saints will laugh and smile cruel smiles and watch the blood drain from her body to puddle on the floor around her like ruby wings—clipped and helpless.

The girl raises her voice, digs deep to find the strength that will keep the Beast at bay, but his shape only presses harder against the red mist. She sees him in bulging shadow. A hand pressed there, then an outline of his face. He is handsome—she thinks—in the kind of way the night can be handsome. The way it swallows and consumes.

"Gráinne." His voice is low, black pine pitch and cruelty. "Gráinne, I know you can hear me. Give me the sword, let me help you."

This is how it always is with the Beast. Promises never kept. If she lets him have the sword he will slash through the mist and come for her. She already tastes the scream on her lips—metal and hot.

"No." A simple word, but one that holds power. "No."

Fingers tighten on the sword. She will not give it to him. Will not be rescued. He has kept her imprisoned for too long. But she is tired; she feels it in the weak muscles of her legs, the way her tendons burn like she's been slashed behind the knees with a jagged blade.

"The sword does not belong to you." He is angry, the heat of him slips through the mist to meet her face and burn her cheeks.

But she does not relent.

She will not.

The sword keeps her safe. And the song.

"It does not belong to you, either," she whispers. "It belonged to him." The bones in the corner, the ones with meat still hanging from them like torn and sullied rags. "And you killed him."

Laughter. It rolls through the mist like thunder and again, she finds it something beautiful. Dangerous. Something she could sink her teeth into.

"Gráinne, you know that isn't true. I would never hurt a fellow man. Please, the sword. Let me come to you."

Her arms shake from the weight of the sword as she raises it above her shoulder, poised for him to come through, to rake claws down her chest and open her to the outside world. But he can't. Not without the sword.

She sings the last notes of the song and watches as the mist hardens, the Beast's shadow growing more and more distant. The bitter taste of victory blooms across her tongue, but is cut short as his voice trills one last time:

"Oh, my little monster, you never last long."

It is morning when she awakens. She only knows this by the bird song that slips through the stones like water. She picks up a piece of charcoal and tallies another day on the wall. Another day of hunger and singing and the sword held tight in her grip. Sometimes she dreams of driving a pike between the cracks in the wall and letting in the sunlight. But she does not have a pike and the sword is only for the Beast. Only for slicing through the red mist to fight him. She knows she will have to eventually. He will grow too powerful, his claws will break through the mist and come for her throat. The last Warden held the sword every third day, just when the song would weaken and the mist would spread. She knows today is the third day. Because when she gets to her feet, cold and bare on the lonely stone, she opens her mouth and no song comes out. Her throat is sore, cracked, and dry. A bundle of sticks left out in the cold and frost. She wets her lips with her tongue, stares at the curtain of red before her that is more like a wedding veil now than a solid swath of velvet.

"Good morning, little monster."

Her bones freeze. The hand around the hilt cramps. She cannot face him. She is not ready, too young and green. A willow sapling staring down the great paws of a wolf. She is no hero. Not like the ones the last Warden used to sing of when he ventured through the mist. Great beings of power who kept the Beast at bay, held back the tearing jaws and sharp teeth and bloody maw.

She is just a girl whose song has died.

"Will you come through to face me or are you a coward?"

Something about his words lights a fire in her belly. It starts as a spark, but as she watches the thinning mist, marks the way his form comes into a more solid shape, the spark fans into raging flames. There's a cry on her lips before she can stop it, the sword swinging high. Her feet move of their own volition. Straight toward the curtain of red and she is washed in its blood.

She braces herself to meet his claws. To feel the rip of them like cold iron through the delicate bones of her sternum. But nothing comes. She blinks away the red and stills. Looks around.

There is no Beast.

Just a boy.

He stands on the far side of the room—a kind of library, she thinks, for there are books on every wall, bound in fine leather and pressed with gold. She sniffs at the air: old paper and ink. Metal, too. Freshly forged. Her fingers tighten around the hilt once more.

"Have you come to kill me, little monster?"

Her eyes flash back to him, watching the way his body moves in the firelight. He is tall, but not as tall as he appeared through the mist. His face is sharp, like someone chiseled him from marble. She always pictured him with claws and teeth and a hide of mangy fur. But his hands are bone white and delicate. The only hint they have ever held a sword are the calluses hardened between the thumb and forefinger. He doesn't wear crude and ruined clothing or tangled and matted fur, but a coat of rich mail, armor polished to a sheen. There is no helm on his head, just a crown of black hair.

"Where is the Beast?" she asks.

"In this room."

Right in front of her, then. For even the Devil can walk about dressed as an angel. Danger always holds beauty.

"It is the third day." She does not state it as a question, but waits for his response anyway.

"The last Warden is dead?"

She nods and is surprised by the sheen of grief that washes across the Beast's face. Almost an expression of regret. He takes a step forward, mail clinking like church bells. A warning.

"May I see him?"

It strikes her as an odd request. Almost brutal, to want to see the corpse of the thing you killed. She shakes her head, raises the sword in hopes he will see it as a warning of her own. But he doesn't. He only inches closer and she catches the smell of him. Ripe apples in autumn and curling smoke from a fire. It has been so long since she's sensed either, that liquid gold taste and homey scent.

"He is dead," she says. "Why would you want to see him?"

The boy—the Beast—stills. One hand frozen midair, outstretched toward the sword.

"Please," he says. "Please, let me hold it. I can help you, Gráinne. It was never my wish to see you imprisoned, to be kept up here like—"

"Like a monster?" Her eyes flash gold. "For that's what you call me, isn't it? Little monster when you yourself are the Beast."

He stumbles back as if hit. "You do not know."

"I know enough to know on the third day I am to come through the mist and kill you with this sword. Every third day until you rise again and the cycle repeats. I know it is my duty to the outside world, to keep them all safe from your bloodthirsty ways. Keep you prisoner until the last of days. A bargaining chip you demanded so many years ago when the world was fresh and young and didn't know of the evil you were capable of."

She does not realize it until she is standing nose to nose with the boy, but every word has brought her closer to him. His eyes are the blue of dead cornflowers in winter. His lips as pale as roses bit with frost. She cannot take her eyes from them and her mind whispers and warns that it is a spell. An enchantment. These were the things agreed to, were they not? By the first Warden. To fall in love with the Beast if one got too close. If one did not slash the Beast to bits before the magic took hold. But her sword hand is already weakening. Her mind is already spinning with the idea of stars colliding behind her eyes when the Beast takes her to bed and spreads her out like the petals of spring's first bloom.

The laughter starts low in his throat. A rumble, the crashing of a waterfall. *Saints above.* His hand is on her waist then, each finger pressing a ghost of him into her skin.

And this is sin.

She knows it. For only sin tastes this good. His lips go to hers, hot and soft and reminding her of summer breezes. For she knew those things once, didn't she? Before she came to this tower, taken by this Beast.

Her mind screams to pull away as he drags her flush against him. But she cannot. Even the sword is barely in her hand. She cannot let go. Even if he is not slayed on this third day, she will have another chance. To keep him subdued by her voice until she can come through the mist again. And this time—his hand reaches to tangle in her matted hair—this time, she will not let him spell her.

"What magic is this?" he breathes against her swollen lips. He pulls away, wiping at his mouth.

She gasps, stumbles backwards, but keeps hold of the sword. "It is yours," she wheezes. "It is how you defeat us."

He pulls at his lips, scratches at his face, suddenly howling like a creature possessed. He rips the breastplate from his chest and turns it around, only breathing steadily again as he watches his reflection.

"What are you afraid of?" she asks, still licking the taste of him from her mouth, her chin, the ghost of his hand still lingering on her wrist.

"Nothing." It is not a word. It is a growl. And then his fist slams into her chest and an invisible string connects to her spine and she is pulled back behind the mist.

In the darkness, on the far side of the red mist, there is a girl with a sword in her hand. And she is crying.

Her throat is raw from singing for two days straight, watching the mist solidify at the sound, and praying to her apathetic Saints that the Beast will be kept at bay. When she closes her eyes, she still remembers the blood. The way it splashed against the village walls and broke like rain over the fields, turning the rye to rot and the wheat to worms.

Her mother's scream, terror in her eyes, reflecting the blaze. The scent of burnt bodies, the turn of fallen apples beneath the trees.

The Beast gave no quarter, slaughtering as it went.

It was only the first Warden who could fight it back into the tower from whence it came. The first Warden who made the mist and the room beyond where every third day, after he sang his voice to ribbons, he would try to fight the Beast. It was the only way to keep it subdued.

Slaying it never caused true death, only made it dormant for a time. And the girl knows the next third day is coming. She will have to use the sword though she is no hero. It has not left her hand, her tendons cramped around the hilt. The thought of facing the Beast once more, now that she knows what he looks like, his handsome face and wandering hands, and blue eyes...The thought burrows into her like a parasite and carves out space there and the space fills with fear.

"Little monster," he croons beyond the crimson veil.

She sees the sheen of his mail through the mist, the hard lines of his legs and muscled arms. What would it be like to kill the Beast for good? To slay him dead forever and return to the village without fear of his teeth and claws? She wonders where he hides them. Teeth behind teeth. Claws contracted into the callused skin of his hands.

"Little monster," he says again.

"Leave me alone," she says, breaking the song if only for a moment. But she takes it up again, weaving the sounds through the mist. He cannot get in. For if he passed through the mist himself, they would all die. He likes the taste of them too much to wait. One foot through and the tower will crumble, stone by precious stone.

And it already seems to be starting. The cracks between the stones are growing, letting in the moonlight. Her stomach growls. Hungry. *So hungry.* She misses the taste of meat between her teeth, the cords of fat and tendon. If she is ever to get out of here alive, it will be the first thing she does. Eat until she is plump and stuffed and supple.

The Beast croons to her, his form slumped beyond the mist. It's only when his whispers of *little monster* turn to sleeping sounds that she lets her own voice rest.

The bones of the last Warden are rotting fast. They always do in this place. The red mist sucking the life from them. She thinks flowers used to grow here, between the stones. Ones the color of spilt blood and milk. But all that remains of them are the thorns.

As the night of the second day fades and the third day is born once more, the girl wonders if the Beast was once ever beautiful. Beneath the pale skin and black curls, maybe there used to be a soul.

She cannot remember what it feels like to have one, though. Not anymore.

It's the screams that wake her this time. She sits up, blinking in the light. *True* light. Her hand goes to her sword and she stands, retreating quickly to the far wall as she takes in the sight of it.

A stone is missing.

The space lets in the light from the outside. She should be screaming, too. The tower cannot come down. But the promise of fresh air is too much and suddenly she has forgotten the sword and her face is pressed into the hole and she is breathing, breathing, *breathing*.

It smells of winter. Of frozen lakes and pine forests. And Saints above, she is hungry. She closes her eyes and smells the cooking fires. The meat. The dripping, hot muscle charred by flame. Yet she doesn't need the fire. Her hunger is so great she imagines sinking her lips against the thew raw, still warm from where it was torn from a body. Her tongue flicks out to taste the air and the screams below quicken.

Her eyes snap open and through the hole she takes in the village. It's not how she remembers it—how long has it been since the last Warden took her? The houses are fewer, their chimney's choking black smoke. The faces on the ground below are stricken and wan, starved and thin. They are all bone. And they are all screaming as they look at her.

Of course.

The missing stone.

The tower is coming down.

But the Beast did not go through the mist, *she* did. How is this possible? Her stomach trembles and her eyes dart about the room, noting the thinning mist.

Not yet. *Not yet.*

She must find something to patch the wall before more stones fall. Her gaze snags on the remains of the last Warden. The bits of ragged clothing still hanging onto a skeleton that otherwise appear licked clean. She buries her fists into them, weaves the tissue back through the bones and shredded cloth and shoves the mess of them into the wall.

The screams only grow louder and his laughter once more trickles through the weakening mist.

"Gráinne, Gráinne." His voice is a tease, a torment, and it curdles her blood.

She backs away from the wall and retrieves the sword from the floor. She does not care if she is not brave. She does not care if she is no hero. She was chosen. She is a Warden, isn't she? Curse his laugh and his form and the spell of lust he puts on her.

She will take him and she will have him and then she will kill him. Once and for all.

The sword cuts through the mist like soft flesh and suddenly she is before him. There are circles beneath his eyes, deep-set and bruised like violets. His hair is disheveled, and he has traded his armor and mail in for a tunic of mulberry-stained linen.

"Do you not wish to fight me today?" she asks, the thrill of early victory already sparking in her chest.

His lips cut a smile, a sad one. Butcher's knife through meat. "I have never wished to fight you, Gráinne."

The words surprise her. "Then what do you wish?"

He sighs, long and heavy. His feet slap bare on the stone as he crosses to her. Closer, it appears he hasn't slept these past three nights. The daybed sprawled before the now-cold hearth is covered in sweat-stained blankets and books whose titles she cannot make out.

"I have always wished to know love," he says finally, so close now his breath is like a hot fog on her skin.

He takes a hand in his, not her sword hand, and studies the love and life lines and how they never cross. She does not pull away.

"My parents always knew what I would become," he says. "It was prophesied over me by a Saint when I was an infant mewling at my mother's breast." He swoops a finger beneath her chin and forces her to look at him. Her knees go soft.

"What have you become?" Her breath is short and untempered, blood coming to pool hot in her stomach.

His lips hover just above hers so that their breaths mingle and dance and a coil of desire is birthed between her legs.

"The Saints always said there would come a Warden who would be the Beast's true downfall." His finger skims across her arm and up her throat, leaving behind a trail of goose flesh. "One who would fall and, only once lust overtook them, be able to slay the Beast forever."

She knows what he is saying. She knows he knows exactly what she is. But a part of her cannot imagine taking him to bed only to rip out his still beating heart and crush it in her palm. All she can think about right now are his hands skimming the curves of her body, his tongue dancing against her own, his breath hot on her ear.

But she keeps hold of the sword.

"Little monster," he growls in the curve of her shoulder and her bones melt.

The sword clatters from her hand but she barely hears it as it hits the floor. And it's then she remembers. Remembers the blood, coursing and thick, the heat and ruin. And Saints above, she is hungry. Her fingers scramble for purchase as she retrieves the sword and lifts it high above her head as the boy stumbles back, surprise etched in lines on his face.

"No." His voice is a desperate breath. An echo of defeat.

She gathers strength and screams, feels the stones shake as she brings the sword down and slices the blade across his sturdy chest. Blood spurts, splashes her face and she licks it greedily. The Beast falls to his knees and slumps to the floor and she shrieks. Not because he is dead. He will rise again just as he always does. But for a while, for the moment, she is a hero and she is safe.

Sword still firm in her hand, the girl slips back through the curtain and goes to sleep. Her lullaby a cacophony of screams below her and the wind through cracks in the stone.

In the darkness, on the far side of the red mist, there is a girl with a sword in her hand. And she is smiling.

The Beast's blood is still thick on her blade. She runs a finger through it and brings that finger to her tongue. He tastes of salt and metal. It is the second day and the screams in the village have grown silent. Now all she hears are whispers. Fearful things traded between fearful tongues. And they have a right to be afraid. For the Beast is not dead.

She can hear him. He shuffles around the room beyond, cursing and stumbling and muttering things she cannot make out. He does not call to her, does not taunt her with words like little monster or that name he keeps repeating. *Gráinne*. It feels like a dream, the name. Like some distant thing she should remember but cannot.

"Gráinne." She runs the name over her own tongue, rolls it around so it clacks against the back of her teeth, yet still she does not feel a connection to it.

The smile fades from her face as she hears the Beast again, moving slowly, his mail and armor clinking. A thorn is digging into her back and she moves to touch it. But it only crumbles into dust. She wonders what would become of the world if the Beast was set free once more. She knows the stories of the times that came before. The way the Beast killed without a second thought. Sank teeth into flesh, burned whole kingdoms and roasted their dead on spits. Her stomach grumbles at the thought and she cannot help it.

Hunger has become a skin she wears.

It is hard to picture the boy—the Beast—in the other room as a monster covered in empires' worth of gore. He seems a soft thing. And she remembers what he said, about being an infant. But that cannot be. For the Beast was not born, but made. A witch's toy fashioned from the earth itself. It is said the Beast started as a single rose the witch plucked. And into it she poured her malice, her own starvation, her craving to be filled with not food, but power. And the Beast sprang forth, curling horns and tangled hair, and legs and arms made from great bundles of dead brambles.

It grew muscle as it consumed it. Learning that to be human meant devouring and so the Beast devoured whatever stood in its path. It killed the witch who made it, for it learned that to be human and take power was only to destroy.

The girl tosses these thoughts around in her mind, trying to make sense of them. Trying to make sense of the boy in the room beyond the red mist. How could he have been born from flesh and blood and yet be the Beast now captured and confined to the tower, kept only at bay by a long string of Wardens?

The thoughts make her tired and her voice cracks, if only for a moment. In the silence, she hears the screams commence below her. A great anger forms in her gut, malignant and hungry. She tears across the room to where the hole is stuffed with bones and muscle and tears it out to bare her teeth down at the village.

Don't they know what she has done for them? What *she* is doing?

The screams grow louder as she gnashes her teeth and gums. Don't they see her wan skin? The way she has given up all good life for them, to keep the Beast at bay?

Something hits her in the face. Juice smears her cheek, and her tongue lashes out for a taste. An apple. Sloughed and rotted but sweet all the same. Her fingers claw at the stone, nails grating. Another taste, another lick.

Her fingers, already bleeding, work to loose another stone. This is wrong, she knows it. The tower must not be weakened. But her stomach calls out to her. To destroy. To take.

Hungry, so hungry.

Just as she loosens the stone, something slashes into her shoulder. Pain bursts behind her eyes and she falls back. An arrow protrudes from her skin, the feather fluttering in the wind. A cry rips from her throat. Animal-like. And suddenly her body isn't hers anymore. She is all anger. All cruel hate and blistering hunger. Another cry and she rips the arrow from her flesh, not shying away as red hot blood bubbles from the wound and stains the thin shift hiding her body from eager eyes.

"Gráinne." It's the Beast on the other side of the curtain of mist. She whips around to face him and sees the dark outline of his form. The curves of his broad shoulders. The shape of him that lights a fire in her core.

"Leave me be," she spits, saliva speckling the floor at her feet. "Leave me be and I will kill you tomorrow."

She bends down to retrieve the sword and slices into her skirt, tearing off the hem. A quick knot at her arm and the blood is staunched; already it is coming slower. But the pain is still here, just as hot as a palm against a stove. She grits her teeth. Moving closer to the mist and opening her mouth. The song spills out. The one she was taught. And watches the mist weaken as the night grows long and dark and full of shadow.

The screams do not abate. And she knows they will be there to greet her in the morning. The third day. When the Beast once more rises and the curtain is weakest, she must use the sword of the fallen Warden to slay him once and for all. She lays her head back against the cold stone, keeps singing, and pictures her mother. The woman with the spider silk hair. The woman who was too beautiful to be real. The woman she killed.

Sometimes, when she's in that strange place between sleeping and waking, she still can remember the feel of the blood on her fingers. It was cold, not hot like all the others. And it was black. Like soot from a fire mixed with water. Her mother screamed and she screamed but hers was not from fear. It was from power. Mother was unkind. Mother was hateful and wrong. Mother did not want her to be trapped in the tower. Killing was the only choice left at the end of the day and though the girl would not admit it, she liked it. The twist of flesh beneath her thin hands, the crackle of bone.

Her song slips slowly out of her and her eyes flutter closed. She will feel blood on her fingers one last time, she decides. Tomorrow, on the third day come again, the Beast will rise, and she will find a way to tear his heart from his chest, still beating, and consume it whole.

It is quite possible the lust will ruin her. The girl wakes with the rising sun that spills in, past what remains of the last Warden. He was young, she thinks. It is hard to remember. He had a kind face and eyes the color of sea glass and she knew his smile. Even when his flesh lay in shredded tears and the sword slipped from his hand, she thought him brave. To go up against the Beast. Like they all did. All the boys with good teeth and handsome faces.

"Little monster."

The Beast sounds more alert. More whole. And she knows he is rising strong again, sure that the wound she inflicted only days ago has now stitched itself anew. Her fingers trail to her own injury, where the arrow pierced her, and finds...

Nothing.

It doesn't make sense. She shouldn't have healed so quickly. No human muscle threads itself back together in such as way. Her breathing turns labored. She pushes herself up from the floor, hands scurrying the stained cloth away and peels down the shoulder of her shift. The skin is fresh. Tight. Pale as the driven snow but healed.

It does not make sense. It makes her mind spin. She reaches for the sword to ground her, but instead she sways heavily against the wall. Tries to calm her racing heart.

No matter. Not now.

The Beast is humming beyond the thin mist. She can make out the whole of him. He has once more left his armor behind. He is a cocky thing, she thinks with a smile. How good it will be to taste him and kill him and taste him again.

Her shoulder can wait. There is blood to spill. She picks herself up away from the wall and takes the sword in her hand. The blade arches across the mist and she walks through, not a speck of red touching her.

The room on the other side reeks.

Leather and books and parchment turning to scents of raw meat and rotten fruit.

"What have you done?" she asks him, sword poised, ready to swing. But that is not how this time will go. This time, she will need him close enough to rip out his heart once and for all.

"What have I done?" His voice is not mocking, rather angry, threaded through with something that reminds her of Mother. Malice and revenge. He peels away the slice of his tunic and she gags.

His flesh is crisscrossed in jagged threads where he tried to sew his own wound together. Pus ekes out between the black strings and she marvels at how real the flesh beneath looks. The muscle, more human than made of twigs and dead bracken. How *human* he has become. She licks her lips.

"You are supposed to heal. Three days." She takes a step closer, notices a bed she has not seen before tucked in one corner of the room.

He laughs. A short, stunted thing like a sawn off limb. "Three days is never enough time." His eyes are hungry things as they take her in and then the sword. Always the damned sword. "Give it to me."

Her fingers curl tighter still and her lips curve into a grin. "Never."

And then she pounces. He is all breath and skin and she needs him. The lust drives her as she moves her body against his and forces him to the bed. This was always how the Beast would be defeated. He himself had said so. Taken to bed by a mortal before being devoured and slain for good. And she can hardly believe she is the one to do it. After all these years. It is her.

She is not the hero she always pictured. Not the thing the bards sing about. Strong and defiant and beautiful. She knows she is none of these things.

But she will kill him.

First, however, she will taste him. For it is always fun to play with one's food.

His muscles go rigid as she throws him to the bed beneath her.

"Gráinne." His voice is thick with it—lust. For her. It fills her with power. And she forgets the sword, lets it clatter to the ground as she wraps her legs around his thighs and holds him there. His fingers come to dance in her hair, and she marvels at the veins in his arms, like tributaries branching out from his heart.

His hot, red, beating heart.

Delicious.

She licks her lips and buries her mouth against his. He tastes of dirt. Of sweat and sunlight and roots beneath the earth. She devours until her tongue floods with blood.

"Gráinne," he speaks again. "Little monster."

"Do not call me that," she says, peeling apart his tunic as his own fingers reach up and pull at the cord of leather at her throat. Her shift falls down around her shoulders and he grins. His eyes gleam hungry.

"What should I call you but your name?" He cups one breast and she moans, moving against him.

"But I am no monster, Beast. You are."

He laughs then, flipping her over on her back and knocking the air from her lungs. "Even after all this time, *that* is what you think?" He takes her wrist between his thumb and forefinger, lifts it to his mouth.

"Then show me the truth," she says as his tongue glides over his skin. "Show me the monster."

Something glints silver and the boy has a knife in his hand. She stills.

No. This is wrong. She is supposed to tear the Beast's heart out; that is the Warden's final job. The reward for lust and hunger. But she cannot stop him, the feeling is too strong.

One who would fall and only once lust overtook them be able to slay the Beast forever.

That is her. It must be.

But the boy is too fast. He brings the blade of his knife down across her skin and she screams, waiting for the blood to spurt and gush against her face. But it doesn't.

Her breath stills.

A single thorn uncurls from the slice in her flesh.

No.

The boy drops the knife and peels back the skin. More thorns, then brambles. Twigs and leaves and dead rose petals. Open, she smells of meat and the metallic tang of blood.

"They said you've grown confused in your age and so I grew careless."

He's bracing her wrists on either side of her head now, but she cannot think straight. There are twigs inside of her. She contains multitudes of the forest.

Mother...who formed her from the earth.

Mother, who she killed.

Blood and meat and fire.

She closes her eyes against the memories but they only grow stronger.

"Gráinne, Gráinne." The boy sing-songs and she feels his hand come to rest above her beating heart.

No.

"The Warden before me knew he could not defeat you. Every time he got this close, it grew too strong. The lust you give men. He lost the sword to you and you shredded his chest open. Can you not remember?"

She writhes, but he is too strong. And she can remember. Moments. Clots of memory. The flash of his smile. His sparkling teeth as he took her to the bed. This bed.

"But the song," she moans. "The song keeps the mist strong."

He laughs, the sound blooming with confidence. "The song weakens the mist, and every third day we are to slip through and slaughter you. Keep you at bay until one of us proves strong enough to finish you once and forever."

No.

Blood and meat and fire.

The taste of it all on her lips. Hungry. Always hungry. The forest she was born from devours. Hungers for the blood and sin and taste of men. She can feel it now, the desire to taste him, to claw him open and slurp down the blood.

It's what she did to the last one. The one who left her the sword. She'd barely left a scrap on him. Saints above, she is so hungry.

Her eyes flash open but his fingers are already knuckle deep in her flesh. Her mouth opens and she screams. It is not a human sound. It is a forest sound. Wind through naked trees. Wolves in the wild. The crunch of bone as a fox kills a hare. She is all of these things and more. She is the death of roses. She is the devourer of men.

She is the monster.

Gráinne knows. The Beast has always dwelled inside. She screams and gnaws and gnashes but the prophets were right. The lust would be her downfall. The boy holds her to the bed, his fingers reaching, reaching and she feels them clench around her heart. She thinks it would be a bloody, horrific end when she first heard of it—when they first locked her in the tower behind the red mist. But instead, it's just a popping of sinew and her heart slips out in this boy's hands. He lifts it in the sunlight and the tower shakes.

Triumph. Defeat. She knows she has felt them both before. But the fear that wracks her body, the way the twigs beneath her human skin shake and tremble, she knows this is neither. The boy crushes her heart, laughing, his lips still rough and red from her kisses.

"Gráinne, little monster. You will never hurt a living soul again."

Her mouth gapes open as the heart turns to ash, as her body seizes and the screams outside turn to cheers.

Blood and meat and fire. She will never know the taste again. She already can feel death spilling thread throughout her bones. The boy moves from the bed and gathers the sword to his chest and then her. He carries her through the mist to the other room. The prison she has called home for so long the years turned her mind to mud.

She can barely make out his shape anymore. But she can smell him. The wound on his chest is oozing. Just one last taste, she thinks. His blood will be the last. But he is too quick. For her, he chooses starvation. And the wind comes through the hole in the wall and licks around her body as her skin turns to char and rot.

She sighs.

In the darkness, on the far side of the red mist, there is a girl with a sword in her hand. And she is dead.

ACKNOWLEDGMENTS

My favorite author and CP, Amanda Havill Adgate, once pointed out that our paths don't always go from A to B. She was right. My path has been quite the winding road and I'm lucky she was by my side through it all. I never thought I'd self publish or be a co-founder of a press. And yet here is Grave Belles' first anthology, featuring incredibly talented female and non-binary authors. As if it could get any better, my sister of twenty five years, Jessica Ferguson, joined Amanda and I in this grand idea of creating a press. She is an avid horror reader and the talented artist who designed the cover... her vision is unmatched.

So, thank you to Amanda and J for walking this path with me. Thank you to all the authors within the pages of this anthology, because without you there would be no book — we are grateful you trusted us with your stories. Thank you to my family for cheering me on and believing in all my wild ideas...I love you so much and am lucky to have you celebrate every big and small win with. Thank you to my writing community for making my debut a success and making my hopes become reality. Your love and support continues to leave me in awe. And thank you to the readers of this book. I hope it creeps the hell out of you. Please continue supporting female and non-binary authors.

Julia Jackson

It has been a joy to create a space where difficult histories and powerful voices can stand together. I am honored to be included among such thoughtful storytellers. Thank you to Julia and Jess, for their support and friendship, and to the authors that trusted us with their words.

I'm grateful to the scholars, writers, and historians whose work on medieval life, especially the lives of women and marginalized people, have helped illuminate the quiet and not-so-quiet struggles that echo into our present. And finally, thank you to everyone who continues to speak, write, question, and resist. Stories like these exist because voices, even when suppressed, have always found ways to endure.

Amanda Havill Adgate

Lately, I've taken my measure of a life well lived by whether I'm spending it pursuing things that would inspire awe in my nine-year-old self. I can think of no better tribute to that quiet and bookish child, already obsessed with all things macabre, than starting an independent press devoted to horror written by extraordinary female and non-binary writers. It is a profound joy to embark on this journey with two talented and equally dark-minded friends. Thank you, Amanda and Julia, for bringing me along on this wild ride.

Thank you to my family for your endless encouragement for my creative pursuits, and making it possible to believe there is no undertaking too ambitious to pursue. To my wonderful, book-loving friends, thank you for sharing my enthusiasm for the printed word and celebrating this new chapter alongside me.

Above all, I am profoundly grateful to Julia, Amanda, and all the talented authors who have contributed to this collection, for entrusting me with the task of designing the face of these wonderful, gruesome, and uncompromisingly truthful stories. And as a reader, thank you for writing them. Without your courage and imagination, readers such as myself would live in a much duller world. May this be the first collection of many dark tales we have the privilege of bringing to print.

Jess Ferguson

About the Authors

Saratoga Schaefer (they/them) is the *USA Today* Bestselling and Indie Press Bestselling thriller and horror author of books such as *Serial Killer Support Group* and *Trad Wife*. Their novels have been featured in *Variety*, *People Magazine*, *Cosmopolitan*, and *Glamour*, and their writing has appeared in Writer's Digest, CrimeReads, and more. Originally from Brooklyn, Saratoga now lives upstate with several needy animals and a haunted clown table. You can find Saratoga on social media @saratogaishere and online at www.saratogaschaefer.com.

M. Stevenson (she/her) is the author of *Behooved*, *This Treacherous Night,* and other novels for adults and teens. She graduated from Brown University (BA, Geology-Biology) and the University of Idaho (MEd, Environmental Education) and has worked as an outdoor educator, wilderness skills instructor, and science teacher. Her poetry and prose have appeared in publications including *Small Wonders*, *PodCastle*, *Barely South*, *Artifice &* *Access,* and *Poets Reading the News.* An avid swing dancer and amateur naturalist, she's often found dancing Lindy Hop or wandering the woods talking to birds and plants. She is based in the Finger Lakes region of New York. Find her online at mstevensonbooks.com

Briana Morgan (she/her) is a horror writer, editor, and author of *The Tricker-Treater and Other Stories*, which won a Godless 666 Award for Best Audiobook. With more than a decade of experience scaring herself and others, Briana has a fresh voice that shines through in her latest book, *The Reyes Incident*, which has sold more than 16,000 copies to date. Her other books include *Mouth Full of Ashes, Unboxed: A Play,* and more. When not writing, Briana loves reading disturbing fiction, playing video games, and spending time with her husband and cat. Find her online at @brianamorganbooks.

C.J. Subko (she/her) is a dreamer and a dabbler. She has a Ph.D. in Clinical Psychology, which makes her highly qualified to think too much. Her short fiction publications include *Inner Worlds* (May 2025), *Small Wonders* (November 2024), *Penumbric Speculative* (December 2025), and *The Deadlands* (April 2025). She is a member of the HWA, SFWA, and Codex. She can be found at www.cjsubko.com.

Ashley Graves (she/her) is a lover of all things horror. Better known as @ash.reads.horror on Instagram, she loves connecting readers with the right horror book. When she's not reading/writing horror, you can find her watching a scary movie, playing a horror game, or running her Bindery Blog. She lives in Tennessee with her three dogs and two cats.

Teagan Olivia King (she/her) grew up in Michigan's wild Upper Peninsula but traded in the stormy shores of Lake Superior for the wind-beaten sandbars of Lake Huron. She holds a degree in Creative Writing from Northern Michigan University and is the author of several works of short horror fiction, as well as the horror novel, *Spit Back the Bones*. She lives in an old farmhouse with her partner, two rescue pups named Remus and Rune, a black cat named Chester, who may or may not harbor the soul of some long-dead deity, and probably some ghosts. Don't worry—as far as she can tell, they're nice.

About the Grave Belles

Amanda Havill Adgate (she/her) is a writer and therapist whose work explores the dark intersections of trauma, memory, and the supernatural. With a background in mental health and a passion for gothic storytelling, Amanda weaves narratives that are both emotionally resonant and hauntingly atmospheric. Her fiction often centers on women navigating grief, isolation, and inherited horror, drawing inspiration from folklore, cult psychology, and feminist theory. She has published short horror stories in multiple anthologies and works with Kristin Dwyer on Breaking The Story retreats. She's also a member of the Horror Writers Association. Amanda lives near the Appalachian Mountains with her feral children and the love of her life, where she balances writing with wild, wonder-filled chaos. Find her on instagram @a.simple.verse.

Julia Jackson (she/her) survived a near-fatal car accident and turned to writing as part of her recovery. She now crafts chilling stories that strip away the masks women wear. She has undergone more surgeries than Frankenstein, prowls the night like Batman, and conjures unforgettable heroes and monsters of her own. Julia independently published Powder & Poison in October 2025, selling 200 copies in its first three weeks. Her work appears in multiple international horror anthologies, and the Horror Writers Association selected her poetry for inclusion in their 2025 annual juried collection. Julia teaches mindful writing at Kristin Dwyer's Breaking the Story Retreat and when she isn't writing, works in corporate communications and watches an arguably unhealthy amount of ghost-hunting shows and horror movies.

Jess Ferguson (she/her) is a graphic designer with a passion for illustration, cryptids, folklore, and the occult. She blends her investigative nature with her desire to explore the beauty of all things strange in order to create cover art that embodies the dark tales within. Naturally, she lives in the woods of Northern Ontario, with her partner and their pack of peculiar creatures. She is a champion of local libraries, loves atmospheric horror stories, and will ensure you don't leave her house without a borrowed book in hand. When she's not at her desk, you won't find her, as she is likely backcountry camping or in her garden hidden under a tangle of tomato vines she refused to thin. Find her on instagram @northernlightsalchemy.

www.ingramcontent.com/pod-product-compliance
Lightning Source LLC
Chambersburg PA
CBHW071436130726
47997CB00006B/2107